Other Books by Lisa Morgan

The Christmas Horse

Sharing Hearts

Mystery Horse

Running Wild

Sharing Hearts

Lisa Morgan

This book is a work of fiction. Names, characters, and incidents either are the product of the author's imagination or are used fictitiously. Any resemblance to actual persons, living or dead, or events is entirely coincidental.

Published in the United States by Seaquine Publishing.

ISBN-13: **978-1482527001**
ISBN-10:1482527006

Sharing Hearts

**A must read for all horse-crazy kids that is hard to put down. The book relates to every aspect of life through the wonderful lessons we learn from horses. I also recommend this book to grown adults like myself...it brings back wonderful memories.*

Holly Hudspeth--Level IV ICP Certified Instructor

DEDICATION

This book is dedicated to Hannah because you remind me both of Candice and Kate combined. Thank you for modeling with your pony Cookie for the cover of this book. I wish you the best with your riding.

Also, thank you to Raina Alexis Kishun for agreeing to model for the cover. You did an awesome job and have a gorgeous smile. You're a natural! Keep up the good riding.

CHAPTER ONE

With the barn door cracked open, Candice Parker slipped inside, her mom close behind. There, standing in the crossties, was the best pony in the world. It didn't matter that they were only leasing him. Today Spirit was officially *hers*.

Candice whispered in awe. "Spirit."

"He's been waiting for you," Kate said. Kate was the true owner of Spirit, but when she outgrew him and got a new horse for Christmas, she decided to lease her pony to Candice, so she wouldn't have to sell him.

Kate handed her a brush. Candice knew what to do; after all, she'd taken riding lessons at Irish Spring Stable for almost a year. Even though Spirit was fuzzy with his thick winter coat, she groomed him until he gleamed. But when it came time to pick up the pony's heavy feet to clean them, he wouldn't budge.

Apparently, Spirit had his own ideas of what he

wanted to do in his timeframe.

While she was bent over, Spirit nudged her, sending her forward and almost onto the ground. She could feel the stares of the others but didn't look at them. If Spirit didn't pick up his feet, she wasn't sure what she planned to do about it.

"He can be naughty sometimes," Kate said, giving her a hand at picking up the pony's foot. "He's going to test you at first, but once you get past it, you'll be fine."

Candice wasn't so sure. She'd dreamed of having her own pony, but never once had the dream involved a defiant pony. Giving him the benefit of the doubt, she decided that his behavior was probably normal. Like Kate said, he was testing Candice.

The pony quickly picked up his foot for Kate. "You have to squeeze here. If he doesn't respond, squeeze harder."

Candice could do this. When he ignored her request on the next leg, she pinched harder. Then harder. To her surprise, with a little help from Kate, he finally picked up the foot. As they reached the last hoof, Candice was able to pick it up on her own. That held promise.

When it was time to place the saddle on his back, however, he dodged sideways. The horses at the riding school never moved, rarely disobeying. For a moment Candice wondered if she could handle the free-spirited pony. She hoped so, because if not she'd hate to disappoint everyone. Candice tried to hide the fact that she was starting to doubt her own abilities. Maybe she'd accepted too big a challenge.

"Let me put the bridle on," Kate said. "He can be tricky."

Oh, great.

It was a good thing Kate offered, considering she had to bribe him with a horse cookie to convince him to take the bit.

Maybe Spirit wasn't for Candice after all, even though she'd done nothing but think of him since her parents first mentioned the lease. He was her only way of riding. It had to work out. Unfortunately, taking lessons at Irish Spring Stable was impossible now since her mom's work laid her off.

"If you'll hold the reins, I can put the bridle on my other horse, Razor," Kate instructed. "Then we can go for a ride."

Candice's heart did a flip. She ran her hand over the pony's sweet face. "We'll have a good ride. I promise," she whispered to the pony after Kate walked away.

Candice tried to ignore her mother, who stepped so close to her that they were practically touching. Sometimes her mom embarrassed her, with her protective way. Candice could stand here and hold Spirit by herself; she didn't need help.

Kate was a couple of years older. Candice needed to act mature if she expected her new friend to want to hang out with a younger kid. If Kate decided not to ride with her, she'd have to ride alone.

Taylor Gibbons, a pretty girl with thick curly brown hair, led her large chestnut pony over to them. "Welcome to our barn," she said to Candice. "If you ever need help with anything, just ask. And by the way, my horse's name is Frankie."

Candice noticed she wore a silver horse necklace around her neck, the same one that Kate wore. It must be a Horse Club pendant, Candice thought, wanting one of her own.

"Thanks," Candice said, appreciating Taylor's welcome, and hoping to sound older than she was. "By the way, I like your necklace."

Taylor fingered the small horse. "It's made out of pewter, and it represents our loyalty to the Horse Club."

Candice was right. "How many members do you have?"

"Two."

Candice's heart sank. With only two members, it would be difficult if not impossible to be included.

"Ready?" Kate asked, interrupting their conversation.

Candice nodded, although she was embarrassed that her mom stood even closer now. Candice led the pony to the barn doors. Her mom opened them farther and the pony didn't hesitate. He lowered his head and overpowered Candice until he reached a patch of green grass without snow along the edge of the parking lot.

Candice pulled, but the pony was stronger. He refused to budge from the grass.

Candice's mom gave a strong tug and the pony lifted his head. He had a gleam in his eye that said he planned to test Candice more. Not a good sign.

Kate and Taylor were already sitting on their horses waiting. If Kate didn't think she could handle Spirit, would she end the lease from the start?

Determined to prove Candice was the right fit for Spirit, she marched the pony to the mounting block. When she stepped into the stirrup, the pony began to walk forward. She pulled back on the reins, and thankfully, her mother stopped him. Leasing Spirit was proving to be a lot different than riding one of the school horses at Irish Spring.

When her mother clipped a lead rope to the side of the bit, Candice felt like a baby. "Mom," Candice lowered her voice. "I can ride him without being led."

"It's for safety," Candice's mom said. "I'm keeping you on a lunge line while you ride. He's not a schooling horse, so he has more spunk than what you're used to. Besides, you've been mostly riding western, and English riding is different."

Horrified about staying on the lunge line, Candice didn't look at the other girls.

"Relax, Candice. If you don't, Spirit will be nervous." Her mom stepped forward to follow the Horse Club girls up the steep hill toward the arena.

Candice wanted to argue but knew it was pointless. Once her mom made up her mind, she wouldn't budge.

When they entered the arena, her mother kept her on the lunge line as promised. She gave Candice a mini-lesson, which was nothing like the riding lessons from her instructor.

"Candice, put your heels down."

Her mom told her that every few minutes. If that wasn't bad enough, she made her remain in a jumping position for a few circles. Aching legs were part of riding, but added to the humiliation of having a line attached to Spirit's bridle in front of girls she wanted to impress, was almost too much to handle.

Then her mom tried to teach her how to post the trot by practicing at the walk first. Candice picked that up easily, until it came to actually trotting. She'd trotted before, only a circle at a time, and posting was difficult. To her surprise, Kate rode up on her horse, Razor.

"What me to show you how to do it?"

Should Candice feel embarrassed, or should she be thrilled that Kate wanted to help her? She chose the latter and watched as Kate trotted around, explaining the rhythm and why Candice would eventually learn to love posting the trot.

When Kate was finished, Candice tried again. She found the beat for two strides but then lost it.

"You'll get it," Kate encouraged and then rode off to join Taylor.

CHAPTER TWO

Kate felt good helping cute little Candice learn to ride. She'd even loaned her a pair of paddock boots and riding pants she'd outgrown. Proper equipment helped for sure.

Kate returned to her best friend Taylor, who was sitting on her horse in the middle of the arena.

"How are you handling all of this," Taylor asked.

Kate shrugged. "Sharing my pony isn't as hard as I thought." That was a surprise to Kate. She expected to experience a lot of jealousy. "I admit, when Candice was grooming Spirit, I did miss him a little. But it passed quickly when I remembered how much I love Razor."

"Good for you. But don't be surprised if something happens to trigger jealousy once the new situation wears off." Taylor was always so wise.

"That's a disturbing thought." Kate needed to change the subject. If she thought too much about

Candice leasing Spirit, she was sure the jealousy, even mild as it was so far, would grow. "Are you going to the Valentine's dance?"

Taylor shrugged. "I'm not sure."

"Maybe that cute guy you like will be there."

"Josh Thompson ... the hottest guy on the show circuit." Taylor blushed and glanced at the sky dreamily. "And one of the best riders I know," Taylor pointed out. "The last time I saw him, which was a month ago at the indoor show, he said 'Hi' to me. I think he's starting to recognize me."

"He should," Kate said. "You've been showing a lot lately."

"But we compete in different divisions." Taylor made a goofy expression, one of which consisted of rolling her eyes back into her head and her jaw dropping open. Then thankfully, her facial expression returned to normal. "I mean, only a couple of guys show hunter jumpers among all us girls. Why do I think he'd notice me?"

Kate laughed and stuck her tongue out at her friend. "Maybe because you're hot. We'll see if he talks to you at the Valentine's party." When Taylor didn't reply, Kate thought she'd made a mistake about Josh being there. "He rides at Irish Spring Stable, doesn't he?"

Taylor's cheeks lightly blushed. "He does. Since Irish Spring is throwing the party, I bet he'll be there."

Kate dropped her stirrups and leaned back, placing a hand behind the saddle to rest her weight on Razor's hindquarters. He didn't seem to mind. "There won't be as many girls at the party as there are at the shows."

"Yeah. Not as much competition," Taylor said.

Kate rolled her eyes. "You thrive on competition, so that shouldn't be a problem. I bet he'll talk to you. He might even ask you to dance."

Taylor's face turned as red as a valentine.

"Look! Candice is posting the trot," Kate said, forgetting that she wanted to avoid the topic of Candice. "Yah, Candice! You're doing it." The little girl held on tight to the pommel of the saddle and kept the two-beat rhythm for a complete circle before she lost her balance and tipped forward. Spirit, the good boy that he was, slowed to a walk to help Candice regain her balance.

"I think deep down you like Candice," Taylor said. "Part of you enjoys teaching, and you want her to be successful."

Amazing. Kate had never thought of herself as a teacher before. "Of course I want Candice to succeed. Without her leasing my pony, I wouldn't be able to keep him." But truth be told, Kate was more jealous than she wanted to admit. Seeing Candice posting the trot successfully, however, excited her. Kate was all about people learning to ride, but she preferred they learn on another pony.

"Kate?" Kate's mom called from the bleachers. "You need to ride your horse instead of sitting in the middle of the arena chatting with Taylor."

Kate huffed and Taylor giggled.

"She's right, you know," Taylor said. "We need to ride so we'll be ready to show together."

They warmed up their horses, but when Kate went to canter, Razor started dancing around. Not sure what was wrong with him, she slowed and asked for the canter again. He lowered his head, tossed it, and bucked.

Kate lost her balance and leaned forward on his neck. If he bucked again, she'd be on the ground.

Before Kate could absorb what happened, her mom appeared in the center of the arena. "Move him forward, Kate. If he tries to lower his head again, jerk it up."

Move him forward? Kate was terrified. She'd never been on a horse that bucked. She didn't want to move him forward; she wanted to get off him. He was much bigger than anything she had ridden.

"Kate, now isn't the time to be scared. Trot that horse as if you have someplace to go."

She inhaled a long, slow breath. Right now she wanted the comfort of her familiar pony, but she needed to be a good role model for Candice. If the younger girl saw Kate afraid, then she'd also be afraid. Kate pushed Razor into a fast trot. When he tried to toss his head, she held her hands in place to prevent him from throwing his neck down. He was stronger, so he pulled against her.

"Kick him!" Kate's mom instructed. "Do not let his head go down or he'll buck again. Keep him on a circle."

Kate focused on her mother's words.

"I want you to work him hard at the trot before you even think about asking him to canter again. You're riding a younger horse now, so you need to pay attention."

Thankful her mom had been riding for years, Kate followed her command. Her mom wasn't Layne Richards, riding instructor extraordinaire, but she'd do in a pinch. At least Razor was responding in a positive manner.

Kate's mom encouraged her to do circles, serpentines, and changes of direction, all to keep his mind focused on work. When he relaxed and was listening to Kate's commands, her mom said, "Now ask for the canter."

Unable to comply with her mom's wishes, she kept trotting. Fear was an ugly thing.

"Kate, you need to canter."

Kate glanced over and saw Candice on her pony, watching intently. Canter, Kate thought, for the sake of a younger, newer rider. Candice needed someone to look up to as a riding mentor, and Kate wanted to be that person. Before she talked herself out of it, she asked Razor for the canter. He moved right into it, without even flicking his tail. He was a perfect example of relaxed and willing.

"Good boy," Kate whispered. "A very good boy." She cantered a few circles, asked for a few trot-canter transitions to make sure he behaved, and then repeated the process in the opposite direction. All the while she kept Razor on a circle at the opposite end of the arena from Candice to keep her safe.

"You can quit with that," Kate's mom said. "I would cool him down, maybe take a short trail ride."

Trail ride? Kate's belly knotted into a small rock.

The U-Turn trail, as Kate and Taylor called it, led to Taylor's farm. If they continued on the trail, it snaked around the backs of a few houses and past a new house that had a barking dog in the backyard. Kate didn't how well Razor would deal with an obnoxious dog, but at least an invisible fence restrained the loud beast. Or so she hoped. They'd never had a problem with the canine before, other than being annoying.

"I don't know, Mom. I've never ridden him outside the arena on Razor, other than walking back to the barn."

Her mom strolled up to her, placed a hand on her knee, while keeping pace with Razor's lumbering walk. "You need to let the fear go. If you don't, it will rule you. Think of the joyful ride you want, and go for it."

Kate glanced at Candice again, who was now walking off the lunge line. She'd graduated from the confines of the rope, at least for the time being. Maybe it was time for Kate to be brave too.

"Okay. I'll take him on a short ride."

"That's my girl." Kate's mom left her side and opened the arena gate.

"Taylor, do you want to go on a short trail ride?" Kate had to take the next step, just like daring little Candice. It was time to unclip the mental limitations she placed on herself.

"Can I go?" Candice asked Kate.

Kate had forgotten about Candice. Of course she'd want to go; she wanted to do everything the older girls did. If she couldn't post the trot yet, much less steer him at the trot without the aid of the lunge line, then she had no business being out on a trail. How was Kate supposed to let her down without hurting her feelings?

"Sorry, Candice, but right now you need to ride in the arena," Mrs. Parker intervened.

Candice frowned at her mother. "I'm perfectly fine riding on a trail. I want to go wherever the Horse Club goes."

"They've been riding a lot longer than you have," Mrs. Parker explained.

Candice's frown turned into a scowl. "I've

been riding for a year."

"Off and on. Candice, we'll talk about this at home." Mrs. Parker clipped the lunge line on the side of the bit again. "For now, we'll return to the barn. At least you get to ride down that trail."

"Do we have to use the lunge line?" Candice asked.

"Yes. Until you can steer at the walk, the lunge line needs to be used outside the arena."

How was it that young Candice wanted to push her limits, without fear, and Kate, who'd been riding for years, wanted to enforce her limits and minimize her adventures?

"Girls, have fun," Mrs. Parker said. She led the pouting Candice out of the ring.

Kate wished she could return to the barn with Candice instead of riding the trail. She hoped Razor would behave. The buck earlier scared her.

"Why don't you go first," Kate suggested to Taylor. If Razor followed, he might behave more.

"Are you afraid?" Taylor asked.

"No." Why did Kate lie? Being honest was important. If she couldn't share her fears with her best friend, then whom could she share them with? "Okay. Yes, I'm afraid."

Taylor stared at her. "That buck didn't look like fun, but you rode through it. When you finished riding, he was soft and gentle. Give yourself a break, Kate. You're learning a lot on him."

"I don't feel Razor and I are ready for a trail." Kate tried not to get defensive, and knew her friend meant well, but she didn't want to be pushed.

"Of course you're ready," Taylor said. "Relax and appreciate the progress you've made today. You did a great job."

That felt good. "Okay. Just ride ahead of me."

"No problem." Taylor guided her horse through the gate and turned down the trail opposite the barn.

Kate followed. Where did Taylor get her unwavering bravery? Without an ounce of fear, she would gallop through a cross country field or take her pony on a hunt. She never seemed afraid.

Eventually they passed Taylor's house, the trail winding down a hill and leading across a grassy bridge. A large pipe ran underneath and a small creek gurgled through it. Razor crossed over as if it were no different from the normal path. Apparently he'd been trail riding before.

They rode deeper into the woods. Up ahead and around the bend was where the dog lived. She knew she should ignore the dog altogether, should ignore the thought he was even there. That way she'd be relaxed and Razor would stay calm. But that wasn't possible. Unfortunately her shoulders tensed. Sensing her anxiety, Razor looked around to see what she was worried about.

As if Kate summoned the dog, the Rottweiler lunged out of his hiding place from behind a bush.

His bark made both Kate and Razor jump, which caused Razor to scoot several feet to the side. Somehow Kate held on and went with her horse.

"It's okay, Razor. He has to stay in his yard." At least she hoped that was a true statement.

The dog seemed to enjoy Razor's reaction and ran toward the end of his territory in the yard. He yelped once, breaking through the fence, and ran like a bullet toward the horses. Even Taylor's horse, Frankie, scooted away.

Taylor turned her horse in a circle to disengage his hindquarters so Frankie couldn't bolt. Good idea. Kate copied her.

"Go home!" Taylor said in a firm voice, pointing in the direction of the dog's yard. When he didn't respond, Taylor deepened her voice and commanded the dog listen.

To Kate's surprise, the dog flattened his ears and scurried back to the perimeter of the yard. He sat by a tree, obviously not wanting to get shocked again. Kate hoped his owner realized he'd broken through the invisible barrier and rescued him soon.

"You were great, Taylor."

"Thanks. I've seen my cross country coach do that before. It works."

Before long they walked out of the woods and the barn came into view. Candice was standing there with her mom nearby, grazing Spirit on a patch of grass.

Kate started chewing on her bottom lip, feeling vulnerable about what happened on the trail. She wished she had her safe pony back. How was she supposed to share her beloved horse with another girl? She about broke into tears but managed to hold them back for now. Jealousy stirred inside her.

CHAPTER THREE

Candice looked up from grazing Spirit to see the girls riding toward her. Nervous, she wrapped her hands a little tighter around the lead rope. Suddenly she had a strong feeling that Kate didn't like her. Candice wanted to be friends, to be a member of the Horse Club. How was she supposed to join the club if Kate resented her?

Kate owned Razor now. Wasn't one horse good enough? Why didn't she focus her attention on her new horse?

Candice promised to take good care of the pony. She had arrived early every morning this week before school to clean his stall, despite her little brother, either complaining, or worse, trying to help. They had to clean the stall again every evening. It was spotless, just as Kate had instructed. Candice even brushed Spirit every day. His coat was shiny, his tail tangle free and gorgeous.

What was there for Kate to dislike? Candice hated feeling judged, disliked, as if she weren't good enough. Well, she was a great fit for Spirit. Nobody else would care for him the way she did. Somehow she needed to prove herself to Kate.

Maybe she needed to ride him better, so Kate would see how perfect she was for him. It would also help if her mother trusted her enough to ride the pony without the lunge line. She was almost nine-years old and could ride without assistance.

"Hi, Candice," Taylor said as they rode up to the barn and dismounted.

The greeting surprised Candice. She wasn't sure why—the girls had been friendly enough—but still, she sensed she was unwanted.

"Did you enjoy your ride?" Candice asked, trying not to show her disappointment. Her mom always told her to make a special effort to be kind to people who didn't like her. She said it made a difference and the kids would often change their minds. So far, Candice wasn't sure the advice was good, but she had everything to gain by trying the suggestion out on Kate and Taylor.

"The ride was relaxing," Taylor said.

That might be the case for Taylor, but for some reason Kate didn't look calm. Her posture was tense and she wasn't smiling. Kate surprised Candice, however, when she said, "You rode Spirit well today."

Candice's pride inflated. Maybe she'd been wrong about Kate not liking her. Or perhaps her mother's kindness trick really did work. Then she reminded herself that it was only one compliment. A brief show of friendliness didn't mean Kate actually liked her, but Candice was thankful for the positive comment anyway.

"Do you want to ride with us tomorrow?" Kate asked.

Candice lit up. "Yes." Her mom stepped behind her. Candice could feel a supportive hand on her back. Trying to fit in with a new group of girls was always hard, especially when they were older.

Kate and Taylor led their horses into the barn and Candice followed with Spirit. She led him into his clean stall, stopping to rub his sweet face before she pulled off the halter. Spirit nuzzled her face and Candice giggled. He mouthed the top of her red hat, the one her grandmother had crocheted, and pulled it off her head. Candice laughed, trying to convince him to give it back. He opened his mouth and dropped the hat by his feet.

"Thanks a lot, boy. Now my hat is full of shavings." Candice patted him. She couldn't get upset. He was the sweetest pony she knew. She picked up her hat and shook it out. "Let me go upstairs and drop some hay for you. Be right back." She loved talking to Spirit. She didn't care if anyone overheard her.

She left the stall, climbed the wooden steps leading to the hayloft, and tossed down two small flakes of hay, which landed on his head accidentally. He'd been eagerly awaiting the hay, so he stood right under the opening. She hoped Kate wouldn't notice what she'd done. She might not like hay all over her pony. But then again, she thought, he was Candice's pony now. At least for the time being.

Candice returned to the stall and dumped feed into his bucket, which he practically dove into. Already she loved him as her own. She needed to make sure Kate knew that, because Candice couldn't imagine giving the pony back.

While Spirit ate, she brushed hay off his face and forelock with her hand.

The older girls walked toward Spirit's stall, not seeing her standing there. She overheard Kate say, "Let's go to my house."

Candice felt a tiny bit jealous. Okay, a lot jealous. She wanted to be friends with the girls, wanted to be included in their activities. They weren't *that* much older. But her mom said there was a big difference between a couple of years. She was probably right, but Candice didn't like being left out. Too bad there weren't other girls her age at the barn, so she'd have someone else to ride with too. Most of the girls who rode there were either in middle school or high school. She was the youngest at the barn. She had no choice but to be friends with older girls.

That was one good thing about riding at Irish Spring Stable. There were kids her age coming and going all day long. The day camps during the summer had eight or nine kids to ride with. But having her own pony was worth giving that up. There would be no more camps this summer. It was too expensive.

“Let’s come up with a plan for the Valentine’s party,” Kate said after they passed by Spirit’s stall. “We need to make Josh Thompson notice you.”

Candice peeked through the bars of the stall and saw Taylor blush.

Josh Thompson. Candice knew him well from riding at Irish Spring Stable. He used to help her before and after lessons with grooming whatever horse she was riding, and he was always there for day camp. She still saw him now and again when she watched her friend’s riding lesson.

Candice covered her mouth to keep from squealing with excitement. Wait until she told Josh that Taylor liked him. That would earn their friendship.

CHAPTER FOUR

"What am I going to do?" Kate asked. She sat cross-legged on her bed, covered with stuffed animals and a lone doll with messy black hair. A pastel quilt bashfully peeked out from beneath the cozy mess. "You were right. It bothers me to see Candice with my pony."

"Why? She's great with Spirit, and he likes her too," Taylor said. She was on the floor, leaning against Kate's white wicker dresser. "Candice is sweet."

"I know. She's adorable."

"Then what's the problem?" Taylor asked. "Don't you like her?"

Kate shrugged. "That's the confusing part. I do like her." Kate knew she didn't make sense, but puzzling as it was, that was how she felt. Her dad often complained that women never made sense; maybe that meant she was a woman now.

"But you don't like seeing someone else show affection to your horse. Is that it?"

Taylor hit the truth straight on.

"Yeah." Kate's throat burned from emotion.

"What are you planning to do?" Taylor asked, leaning closer to Kate.

Why did her friend always have to be so direct? Sometimes it really got on her nerves. Like now.

"I don't know," Kate said, irritated. "I admit, I need to learn to deal with Candice leasing my pony. The situation isn't her fault."

Kate wished she could keep Spirit without having to deal with a lease. According to her mother, though, time was the issue, not money. If they didn't lease the pony, then they had to sell him. One horse was hard enough to manage in her mother's busy schedule. Kate's father was a doctor and was barely home as it was. He didn't have time to help maintain a horse.

Kate didn't mind doing all the work; in fact, she loved it. But her mother still had to drive her to the barn, be present in the arena while Kate was riding, and cleaning one stall twice a day was time consuming enough. Even though her mother worked from home for a marketing research company, she needed to be working instead of taking care of horses. Kate considered owning one horse a gift, two a blessing.

"Maybe you should reconsider selling Spirit,"

Taylor reasoned. "That way you wouldn't see someone else riding and taking care of him."

Kate shrugged. "I can't stand to let him go, to never see him again."

"I understand, but maybe holding onto him is harder than letting go."

Kate didn't think so. Besides, her mom was just as attached to Spirit as Kate was, even if she avoided admitting the truth. They both would miss him.

"I could ride at a different time than Candice," Kate suggested. "That way I won't see her with Spirit."

Taylor frowned and shook her head. "Then Candice would have to ride alone. That's not much fun for her. And at some point you'd run into her, feeding Razor or riding." Taylor tossed her hands in the air. "Like I said, maybe you should sell him so you don't have to keep hurting."

Kate started chewing on her lower lip, a nervous habit meaning something was bothering her. "Selling him isn't the answer. I can't run away from this. Somehow, I need to deal with my jealousy."

Taylor grinned. "True. How are you going to do that?"

Kate had no idea. "Maybe I'll get used to it eventually." Even as she said the words, she knew that wasn't likely to happen. She decided to change the subject. "Let's talk about Josh Thompson?"

"What about him?" Taylor blushed again.

"Let's say fifty people show up at the Valentine's dance," Kate said. "Some will be adults, but the rest will be girls. How are we going to get him to ask *you* to dance?"

"Why do we have to do anything? If he wants to dance with me, then great. If not, it's his loss."

How could Taylor always be so frustratingly levelheaded? From the way she blushed at the mention of Josh's name, she definitely liked him. "Why leave it to chance?"

"Why not?" Taylor asked.

Kate threw a pillow at her. "You're so romantic," she said sarcastically. "Every girl in that room will chase after him. As competitive as you are, why would you allow them to steal his attention away? Think about it. Imagine dancing with him."

She'd hit a nerve with her friend, whose face was now bright red.

"You know you want to be close to him, in his arms."

Taylor plucked an overstuffed teddy bear from the floor next to her. She chucked it at Kate. "It's a dance. There isn't going to be any romantic kissing or close dancing. Give me a break. We're still kids."

Kate rolled back on the bed laughing.

Taylor tossed another stuffed animal at her, this time an elephant. "My mom would ground me for a year if I got cozy with a boy."

"Point understood," Kate said. "We need to get him to notice you above all those other girls, and to ask you to dance. Casually."

"Maybe you're the one who likes him," Taylor said. "You seem fixated on him."

Actually, Kate did like him but she'd never admit it. She'd seen the way her friend blushed whenever Kate said his name. They'd promised each other never to allow a boy to come between them, and jealous or not, Kate would hold up her end of the agreement.

"While we're solving the world's problems," Taylor said, "why don't we discuss a plan to help you face your fear of Razor."

Kate stuck her tongue out at her pushy friend. "I'll be fine. The more I ride him the safer I'll feel."

Taylor raised her eyebrows. "You've been dealing with fear since you've first started riding. What are you afraid of?"

"Falling off."

"What's so bad about that?"

Kate gasped. "I could think of a bunch of bad situations, none of them I'd want to experience."

"My mom says when you focus on fear, you aren't trusting. You'll bring bad things to you to match your thoughts."

Kate rolled her eyes.

"Turn the situation in a positive direction,"

Taylor suggested. "That's how you got Razor. You wanted him so much that even when another woman planned to buy him, he ended up on your front lawn Christmas morning."

Kate remembered the excitement of hearing a horse whinny, remembered looking out her window to see him standing there.

"So we need to work on turning your fear around."

That was harder than it sounded.

"We can start by trotting over a few small fences," Taylor suggested.

Was she joking? "Not a chance," Kate said. "Layne needs to be there."

"Why? You've jumped Razor before in lessons," Taylor reasoned. "Just trot over a pole; you don't have to jump anything big. It'll build confidence. Look how great you handled the trail ride."

The trail ride wasn't a good example. Kate didn't view it as a successful venture

CHAPTER FIVE

One day after school, Kate and Taylor entered the barn. Kate, determined not to be jealous, wanted to try turning her thoughts in a more positive direction. But she didn't get far. Kate gasped and stopped dead in her tracks.

Handmade Valentine's cards and cutout hearts covered Spirit's stall. A small poster hung in the center of the artwork with pink handwriting. *Be My Sweetheart Pony*.

Kate grabbed hold of Taylor's elbow, rushing her through the barn and out the backdoor. They were standing alone on the patchy, snow-covered walkway.

"How am I supposed to get over my jealousy when she's personalized his stall?" Kate asked, trying to fight off panic. "She did that just to bother me."

Taylor held Kate's shoulders still and looked

straight into her eyes, as if she were a parent. "This has nothing to do with you."

"Of course it does. She's trying to make me jealous."

Taylor shook her head. "No. She isn't thinking about you. She's showing her love for the pony by making him things."

Why did it hurt so much?

"Kate, it's good she loves him. That's what you want, right?"

Sure. "I want her to take good care of him. I didn't mean for her to fall in love with him, or to flaunt it in front of me."

Taylor let go of Kate and sighed so loudly it made Kate almost physically sick to her stomach.

"Sorry to frustrate you," Kate said.

Taylor drew in a long breath before responding. "Like I said, this isn't about you. She didn't wake up this morning wanting to force her love for Spirit in your face. Come on, Kate."

Kate poked out her lower lip. What Taylor was saying made sense, but her heart was aching. "I can't do this."

"Then sell him."

Kate glared at her friend. How could she be so mean?

As if Taylor read her thoughts, she said, "I'm not trying to hurt you. Those are your two choices, and I recommend dealing with the jealousy. Give yourself a day, maybe a week, to feel it. Then let it go."

Kate inhaled a long, deep breath. "You're right." She walked back into the barn, ignoring the ripping pain in her chest, and she entered the tack room, which was located right across from Spirit's stall. She would tack up her new horse and enjoy riding him.

Candice bounded into the tack room behind her. "Hi! I'm so glad you're here. I'm ready to ride with you."

How could she be so bubbly all the time? Kate resisted making a snappy remark. Remembering Taylor's suggestion to turn the situation into a positive one, Kate forced a smile. "We'll be saddled up in no time."

"My pony is brushed and ready to go."

My pony. Kate tried to ignore the ache that word caused.

"Guess what?" Candice asked, bouncing in place. "My mom said I could try riding more off the lunge line today. I'm ready."

"I'm sure you'll do a good job," Kate said, trying to let the jealousy go.

Candice beamed. It was obvious the little girl needed positive feedback from Kate. She was probably feeling uncertain about the new situation too.

Kate bit back the pain and said, "I like your

decorations. Looks like you worked hard on them.

Candice smiled wide. “Thanks. It took me two days to make those. I hope Spirit likes them.”

“I’m sure he does,” Taylor said, flashing Kate an approving nod.

With the younger girl in the barn, the dynamics of the Horse Club were changing, even if they didn’t invite Candice to join. Just having her there tested Kate’s patience.

Kate and Taylor left the tack room and hurried to saddle their horses. Within twenty minutes, Kate, who was always the last one to the mounting block, walked Razor out of the barn. The other girls were mounted and waiting.

She climbed on Razor. He stood perfectly still, unlike Spirit. Kate loved having a well-trained horse, not that Spirit was untrained, but sometimes his manners needed improvement.

They started walking across the parking lot when Kate noticed something different about Candice. “You aren’t on the lunge line.” Kate knew Candice wanted off the line, but hadn’t expected her to ride independently outside the ring after just a few times riding Spirit.

Candice sat a little taller.

Mrs. Parker said, “She’s steering better now. And your mom gave us anti-grazing reins to keep him from pulling his head down to eat grass. I feel better letting Candice off the lunge line if I know he won't unseat her."

"I had to use them the first year I rode him," Kate said. "They work well. He can't yank his head down."

"Can I walk up the trail first?" Candice asked.

"Honey, I think Razor needs to go first," Mrs. Parker said. "He's bigger and walks faster."

"It's all right, Mrs. Parker. Razor needs to learn patience." Kate could relate to that. "I don't mind following." She felt safer having other horses in front. Her annoying fear issue was always hiding just under the surface. Speaking of fear, she hoped Taylor would forget that they were supposed to jump today. Kate's belly knotted.

When they reached the top of the hill Kate saw her mother in the Lexus. She was probably working on her laptop, which drove home the fact that time was an issue for her mom. She was always so busy, but here she was, waiting for Kate while she rode.

Instead of spending the beginning of the ride in the middle of the arena talking to Taylor, Kate got right to work. The quicker she got started, the faster she'd finish. She warmed up Razor, varying the workout so he wouldn't feel the need to buck today. She'd had her fill of that.

Kate couldn't help notice that Candice was still riding off the lunge line, practicing steering. The little girl was brave. Apparently she pressed her mom until she got her way and was riding alone.

Her mother remained close by, Candice riding in a circle around her mom. She was willingly pushing her limits to better herself.

Kate wished she could do that.

When she thought Razor was calm enough, she asked for the canter. He listened but she had to ride him every step to keep him from throwing his head down. She returned to trotting and worked him harder. She noticed her mom was out of the Lexus now and standing along the fence watching. She was obviously concerned about Razor's behavior but she was letting Kate handle the situation.

Eventually he cantered calmly. That's when Taylor struck with her fix-it attitude. "Let's jump."

"I'm good," Kate said.

"Remember what we talked about?"

Like Kate could forget.

"Just trot over the little cross rail. No big deal."

When had Taylor become Kate's trainer? Kate shook her head.

Taylor ignored her response and started trotting over jumps, beginning with the low cross rail. Then she progressed to a larger cross rail with a flower box in front. She picked a line, trotted in and cantered out the second jump. She was having a blast. Kate was more than envious.

Kate glanced over at Candice, who was back on the lunge line for her trotting lesson. She could help the little girl with posting the trot again, but that would be avoiding her annoying fear issue. Would ignoring it be so bad?

Taylor picked up the canter and jumped a line of fences, then a small course.

Kate wanted to have fun too.

She drew in a deep breath, then picked up the trot. She was going for it.

Razor trotted eagerly to the base of the jump, but when he landed awkwardly, he started tossing his head. Before she could react, he yanked his neck down. And bucked. Kate lost her balance and collapsed on his neck. Thank goodness he'd raised his head. When he tossed it again, Kate kicked him, yanking his head up.

"Stop that," Kate yelled louder than she wanted.

"Push him forward, Kate!" her mom hollered.

Kate couldn't move him forward. Her insides felt frozen. Instead of listening to her mom, she stopped Razor and got off.

"What are you doing?" her mom asked. "Get back on him. Don't let him win."

"I need Layne," Kate said, her lower lip trembling.

"Layne is on vacation for the next two weeks. You've got to ride Razor."

Kate shook her head. "I can't."

"Someone needs to, and I'm not dressed for riding." Kate's mom looked at Taylor.

Would her mother actually humiliate Kate by asking her best friend to ride Razor?

Her mom scurried away from the fence, through the small opening in the gate, and into the arena. “If you don’t ride him, Kate, someone else will have to. Get on your horse.”

Kate almost wished she were on the lunge line like little Candice was. Safe and sound. Candice stopped riding and was watching Kate now. Great. She looked like a chicken even to a child.

Reluctantly, Kate led Razor over to the mounting block. With dread racing through her body, she placed her left foot into the stirrup. All she had to do was take one baby step at a time. That’s all. No one could push her into doing something other than what she wanted. She glanced at Candice again. Candice gave her a thumbs-up. How embarrassing.

Kate had to ride, if for no other reason than to keep the respect of a younger rider.

She climbed onto Razor and cued him to walk. Maybe she hadn’t worked him hard enough on the flat, or maybe it was the cold weather. Spring wouldn’t be here soon enough.

“Forget jumping until Layne can help you,” her mom instructed. “Just work on transitions, especially trot to canter.”

Thankful to her mom, Kate had a reason not to jump, at least for now.

Scared, she asked Razor for the trot. He was a bit too forward and hypersensitive. She should have recognized the tension in him earlier before she'd jumped. Part of getting to know him was learning his warning signals and knowing how long to work him before she moved to the next phase.

She practiced transitions and serpentines until he was much calmer, but even then she didn't trust him.

Once she felt they achieved enough for the day, Kate started to cool him down. Truth be told, she couldn't wait to dismount. She wasn't bonding with Razor how she'd hoped.

"Look, Kate," Candice said, posting the trot. She maintained the rhythm for almost two circles before she lost it again.

"Way to go, Candice." Even though Kate was jealous of the little girl, she was happy for her success. Their age difference kept them from ever being friends, but she had to admit, Candice was a sweet girl.

CHAPTER SIX

The next morning Candice's brother, Colin, decided he no longer liked going to the barn before school. She didn't really blame him. After all, Spirit was her pony, not his. What benefit did he get from cleaning a stall?

As far as six-year-old brothers went, he usually wasn't too bothersome. Sometimes, though, he tried to ruin what she loved. Until today, he wanted to help too much with the stall. Spirit was Candice's horse and she wanted to do everything herself. But now Colin was cold and bored, and he wanted to leave.

Her mom pulled her aside. "Give him a job to do. That way you get finished faster."

"He cleans the stall all wrong."

"What does Colin do differently?" her mom asked.

"He mashes the manure and spreads it out. It's

harder to clean." Honestly, she didn't want her brother in the stall. "Why can't he find something else to do?"

"Candice, it's cold out here. He needs to keep busy to keep warm."

Why couldn't he wait in the car? Did she have to share everything with her brother? Didn't a girl deserve to have something to call her own? She already had to deal with Spirit belonging to Kate. It seemed like whatever she cared about she had to share.

"Give him a job. If you make him feel helpful, he'll feel good about himself and leave you alone in the process," Candice's mom reasoned.

"But he makes more work for me."

"Find something he's good at."

All this discussion made them late for school. Nobody was happy about that, especially her mother because she had to park the car in order to go inside to sign them in.

Things grew worse after school when it was time to ride Spirit. Not only did Kate and Taylor not show up but also Colin was antsy. He usually went to a friend's house on the days Candice wanted to ride, but not today. His friend had karate. That meant Colin had to join them at the barn.

Whenever he got bored, he whined, saying that he wanted to go home. Worse yet, he often looked to Candice for entertainment. Either way, his behavior distracted and slowed her down.

By the time she tacked up and rode to the arena, Colin was completely restless. She didn't blame him. His soccer games were boring to watch too. Right now, though, she wanted to concentrate on riding. The quicker she learned how to post the trot, the sooner she could ditch the lunge line altogether.

Unfortunately, the entire lesson she rode on the dreaded line. Candice, determined to learn, focused on the rhythm of the trot. Whenever she missed a beat, frustration knotted her insides. She wished she could just enjoy the ride and relax, but she wanted Kate's approval, wanted Kate to think Candice was the perfect fit for Spirit.

If she improved her riding, Kate would want her to continue to lease Spirit. The thought of losing him was too sad to think about.

"Candice, relax. Smile while you're at it," her mother said.

"I'm happy, Mom. I'm just trying to ride the best I can. I want to learn how to post the trot so I can ride without this rope attached."

Candice's mom stopped Spirit. "Ah, honey. Just let it happen. It takes a while to learn."

Candice looked away from her mother. Colin was on the ground, pushing the arena sand into a pile and making a moat around the mound. At least he found something to do instead of running around, spooking Spirit.

"You can't make those girls like you," her mother continued to say. "Just be yourself. You have a lot to offer. If they recognize that, then fine. If they don't, that's not your problem."

"It's my problem if I have to ride alone all the time. This stinks." Candice glanced around the quiet arena. She missed riding with Kate and Taylor more than she imagined. "Riding is supposed to be fun, done with friends. I don't have any at the barn."

"Give it time," her mom said. "Kate and Taylor will come around. And who knows? Other girls your age may decide to board their horses here. You never know."

Her mom was usually right, but Candice doubted new girls would show up at the barn.

"This is about riding, not about making friends," her mom said.

"It's about both, Mom." Candice nudged her horse to walk. "The faster I learn to trot, the faster I can ride with the older girls. I want to go on trail rides with them. Most of all, I want to be asked to join the Horse Club."

Her mom didn't argue. Instead, she continued helping her post the trot. Candice practiced repeatedly, and Spirit, patient beyond belief, eagerly maintained a steady pace. He seemed willing to help her too. Her bouncing around on his back had to be uncomfortable for him.

By the end of the ride she was able to trot several circles while keeping the rhythm. Once she even let go of the pommel of the saddle with one hand. Eventually she hoped to have enough balance to release both hands and steer. Then she'd be well on her way to riding without help, to riding around the ring with the Horse Club girls. Overall, she was happy with her success.

When they got back to the barn, however, Candice did a double take at the dry erase board. Someone had written a note in pretty, neon pink handwriting. *I love Spirit.*

Immediately Kate's name popped into mind. She must have stopped by the barn to feed early. But why would she write that? Kate owned Razor now.

Candice grew angry. He was her pony. Did that mean Kate was changing her mind about leasing him to Candice?

Her mother stopped beside her. "I'm sure the note doesn't mean anything other than Kate is missing her pony."

Tears burned her eyes. "I thought he was my pony."

"He is temporarily, but he still belongs to her. She might be needing reassurance that you aren't taking him over."

Candice frowned. She didn't understand all of this. She looked at the note again and sadness filled her heart.

"Mom, I love Spirit. I can't lease him without loving him. That's not fair."

"I know, sweetie. Can you find a way to remember Kate owns him, and that she's being nice by sharing him with you? She's giving you a gift."

Kate didn't think she could speak; she wanted to cry. How could her mom take Kate's side? Was Kate being mean by writing that note, or was she missing Spirit like her mom said? Why couldn't Kate focus on bonding with Razor instead of Spirit?

CHAPTER SEVEN

Kate and Taylor finally ran into Candice at the barn. They had opposite riding schedules all week, mostly because Kate took gymnastics twice a week. Juggling that with riding and schoolwork proved to be difficult most days.

Today was a special day, though. According to the lease agreement, it was Kate's day to ride Spirit. She rode him twice a week—once during the school week and once on the weekend—to keep him well tuned. Even though he'd never jump again because of arthritis, he was still able to walk, trot, and canter around the soft arena. He could even walk on a trail ride, which worked for Kate because she wasn't afraid to take him outside the arena as she was Razor.

Actually she was surprised to see Candice at the barn today, since it was Kate's day to ride.

"Hi, Candice." Kate poked her head inside

Spirit's stall to see what she was doing.

"I brushed him for you." Candice smiled so big it seemed almost fake.

Kate chewed on her lower lip. She loved brushing Spirit and preferred Candice not take that away from her. She reminded herself that she owned Razor, who needed brushing too. Spirit was the only horse Candice had to groom. Kate needed to be fair.

"Thanks. That was sweet." Forced or not, Kate wanted to be friendly. She pushed open Spirit's stall door farther and slipped through. Spirit, glad to see her, pushed his head against her chest and rubbed his itchy face on her puffy blue coat. Kate laughed. "Come here, silly pony." She scratched his forehead hard with her gloved hands. He lowered his head, eager to receive the love and affection.

"Do you want to lead him out and cross tie him?" Kate asked, wanting to be generous and caring. She needed to appreciate what she had, not what she didn't have.

Candice's face lit up. She slipped Spirit's halter on and led him from the stall. Kate handed her a cross tie and encouraged her to clip it onto his halter. Being kind felt good. She had to learn to put her jealousy aside and to tap into her generous nature. It was there, begging to escape.

Kate left them alone and walked into the tack room. She looped Spirit's bridle over one shoulder and scooped the saddle and blanket onto the opposite arm. She couldn't wait to ride her familiar pony. She'd had enough of dealing with the fear of riding a new horse. She also looked forward to riding Spirit on a trail after working him in the ring.

Grateful she had a second horse to ride to regain her confidence, she wondered what she would have done had she sold Spirit.

Kate walked out of the tack room and set the saddle blanket on Spirit's back. He seemed eager for Kate to ride because he didn't scoot to the side as he normally did. He even stood still when she placed the saddle on his back. What a treat. When it came time for the bridle, though, she was certain she'd still have to bribe him with a horse cookie. Some things never changed.

"I need to learn how to put his bridle on," Candice said.

"It's tricky. You can't give up and you have to be quick. Like this." Kate demonstrated, letting Candice help. He only opened his mouth for a fraction of a second to take the cookie.

"I did it," Candice exclaimed.

"Yes you did." Kate led him through the aisle, out the barn doors, and to the mounting block, where Taylor was waiting for her on Frankie. Kate tightened the girth, and then climbed on. Spirit even stood still to be mounted. What was going on? Was he happy to see her, or was Candice working magic with him?

"Are you coming up to the arena to watch?" Taylor asked Candice.

Candice shrugged.

Annoyed, Kate stared at her friend. Why had she invited Candice to join them? Kate wanted to enjoy her pony without having to share him. She wanted to lose herself in the moment without the stress of worrying about hurting the little girl's feelings.

Kate's mom overheard them as she headed toward the Lexus. "That's a great idea. Hop in, Candice, and I'll give you a ride."

Candice looked at her mom for approval. When her mom nodded, Candice said, "Thanks, Mrs. Patrick." She walked across the parking lot and climbed into the car.

Kate's mom opened the car door, but before she climbed in, she flashed Kate a warning look. Apparently she wanted Kate to be kind. They had a long discussion last night about that very subject.

"We'll meet you up there, Mom," Kate said. Didn't her mom know she was trying hard?

As they rode the horses up the hill, Taylor, leading the way as usual, twisted around in her saddle. "How are you doing?"

Her friend was checking in with her. Kate had spent a lot of time last night, after the discussion with her mother, talking to Taylor about how to handle the situation with Candice. She was surprised to learn that Taylor felt the same way as Kate's mom. They both thought she needed to let Spirit go emotionally and to allow herself to bond with Razor. Again, that was harder than it sounded.

Once they reached the arena, Kate was eager to exercise her pony, so she got right to work. She was surprised at how tiny his stride was at the walk compared to Razor's. When she picked up the trot she was amazed at how much shorter and quicker his step was. Once she adjusted to the differences between the two horses, she enjoyed the familiarity of him. He was safe. To her surprise, he was even a little bit boring. That was shocking.

That meant on some level she liked riding Razor. Sure, she was afraid of him somewhat, but part of her liked the challenge. That was valuable information.

No one needed to push her to do more on Spirit. Eagerly she worked him through all three gaits. She'd even jump him if he were able.

She was enjoying Spirit so much that she'd forgotten about Candice. Kate looked around until she noticed the little girl leaning against the arena fence, frowning. Why was she angry? Then Kate realized she had a wide smile plastered on her own face. The grin was pure joy from riding her beloved pony. No wonder Candice was upset. She didn't want to share Spirit anymore than Kate did.

What a disaster.

Be understanding, Kate reminded herself. She rode up to Candice, who looked surprised to be included. “Do you want to cool him down?”

Candice nodded. “But I don’t have a helmet.”

Kate slid off the pony. “You can use mine. It might be a little big, but we can adjust it.”

Kate shortened the stirrups to the top hole. When she finished, she handed Candice the helmet. Candice placed it on her head and Kate adjusted the chinstrap.

“There you go,” Kate said.

Candice’s blue eyes met Kate’s. “Thanks.”

Kate nodded. Generosity did feel good when she allowed herself to embrace it. Another surprise. She was learning so much lately. Layne had said she would learn more than riding by buying a bigger horse. Guess she was right.

At first Kate walked next to Candice. It was fun to feel like a big sister, but then she realized Candice could handle walking on her own. She stepped away from the younger girl and stood by the mounting block.

Candice sat taller and concentrated on steering Spirit around the jumps. She made an obstacle course, which was good for keeping Spirit’s mind engaged.

“You’re doing a good job with him,” Kate said. “You’ve made a lot of progress in a short amount of time."

Candice didn't speak but she grinned.

After ten minutes, Taylor finished riding. "Are you ready to go on a trail ride?"

Kate realized her mistake instantly. She should have warned Candice ahead of time that she wanted to take Spirit on the trails.

Candice frowned.

Kate was trying but she always seemed to mess up.

"I'm sorry, Candice. I should have let you know." Actually, Kate should have respected Candice enough to ask if she minded. But she knew the answer. Candice would mind, and then Kate wouldn't get to go. This way, by not asking, Kate got to trail ride with her friend.

Candice remained quiet.

Kate felt bad for the girl. Was she also upset because Candice wanted to ride on the trails with them? The brave little girl always wanted to do things she wasn't ready for. Deciding it was the latter, Kate said, "You'll be able to ride on a trail someday too." Candice still didn't speak. "We won't be gone for long. Promise."

Candice slipped from the saddle and landed on her feet. She removed Kate's helmet and silently handed it back.

"Thanks. Will you be at the barn when we get back?"

Candice shook her head.

"I can feed him then. Maybe we'll see you tomorrow." Kate was trying but she'd hurt Candice. What was she supposed to do? She needed Spirit just as much as Candice needed him. No one could expect Kate to just buy another horse and walk away from loving this one.

Without a word Candice climbed over the arena fence and headed up the small hill to the Lexus. She opened the door and disappeared inside.

Kate readjusted the stirrups and mounted Spirit.

"Ready?" Taylor asked.

Kate nodded, pushing the guilt aside. It would feel good to ride Spirit on the trail without Candice watching. Kate needed a confidence boost after everything she'd been through with Razor lately.

Taylor started for the gate first but Kate held up her hand.

"I'll lead for once," Kate said. Too bad she felt safer on her pony than Razor.

CHAPTER EIGHT

Mornings were growing rough. Cleaning the stall had started out fun at the beginning of the lease, but January mornings were cold. Candice's brother was becoming even more tired of the ritual. The newness had worn off for all of them.

Candice scooped a mound of manure into the muck bucket. Her feet ached despite the warm boots her mom had bought. Her fingers were numb though she wore waterproof ski gloves on her hands. Even Spirit seemed testy.

She tossed another pitchfork of manure into the muck bucket. The poop was frozen solid and thudded when it landed against the plastic. Definitely, the glamour of leasing a pony was wearing off.

The afternoons had been snowy and too wet to ride in the arena. She was doing all this work without the benefits of riding.

"Hurry up, Candice." Colin had reached his limit dealing with the cold. His ears were red because his hat had slipped too high on his head.

"Why don't you wait in the car?" Candice asked, trying to protect her little brother. Even if he annoyed her sometimes, she didn't want him to be cold. It was downright frigid outside.

"I'm sick of coming to the barn. Can't we leave?"

"We can't. I have to finish cleaning the stall first." Remembering her mother's suggestion to give him a job, Candice said, "Will you help me? We'll finish faster."

Colin picked up the plastic pitchfork and tossed it against the wall. "I want to leave. I'm sick of this pony."

Their mom squeezed through the small opening in the stall door. "Come on, guys. Let's get the job done as a team. Then we can climb into the car and warm up."

Colin groaned. "But I want to go now. It's too cold out here."

"You can wait in the car if you want," their mother said. "Otherwise let me zip up your coat more."

Colin gave up complaining. He must have realized there was no other choice but to finish the barn work. The stall still required cleaning along with the water buckets needing fresh water.

"Colin, can you stick the hose in the water bucket and turn it on?" Candice asked.

He left the stall and shoved the hose through the bars at the top half of the stall. When he turned on the faucet, the hose spurted a few times.

Candice grabbed the hose before it snaked out of the bucket and sprayed them. Getting drenched in twenty-degree weather didn't sound like fun. Thankfully the water trickled out slowly since the hose was half frozen.

Their mom picked up the pitchfork and power cleaned the stall at record speed. "Finished," she said. She lifted the bucket and carried it out of the stall, placing it on the wheeled cart. Candice didn't watch but knew her mom pushed it out into the slippery parking lot to empty the bucket into the dumpster.

When both water buckets were full, Candice removed one of her gloves to close the nozzle on the hose. "Colin, can you turn that off."

He groaned but did what she asked. Candice pushed the crunchy hose back through the bars so he could roll it up.

"Are we ready to leave?" her brother whined.

Candice glanced around the clean stall. Spirit was happily munching his hay and he'd already eaten his feed. "We're ready."

"Finally." Colin dashed toward the barn doors, leaving the hose sprawled on the aisle floor. He disappeared through the small opening between the doors.

Candice shut the stall door and wrapped the hose back up.

Even though her brother annoyed her most days, she appreciated that he came to the barn every day to take care of her pony. He could make the overall experience miserable if he didn't cooperate.

Candice met her mom coming out of the feed room, where they also stored stall supplies. "Let's get in the car," her mom said.

Right now all Candice wanted was the heater to blast her with warm air. In a rush to get out of the cold, she squeezed through the opening between the doors. Her foot slipped on the ice just outside the door and she lost her balance. Thankfully her mother grabbed her arm.

"Careful." Her mom helped her regain balance, and then she pulled the heavy barn doors shut. She reached for Candice's arm again and held onto her until they reached the car. After they settled inside, her mother cranked the heat on high. Thankfully the air was still somewhat warm from their earlier drive to the barn. Too bad Candice didn't begin to thaw out until they pulled into the drop-off circle in front of the school.

She must really love Spirit to be doing all this work during the coldest months of the year. If she could hold on a little longer, spring would be here.

Until then, Candice didn't know if she wanted to ride much. It got dark early, and the sun went down before she finished riding.

"Have a good day," their mother said.

The kids climbed from the car and waved goodbye.

By the time their mother picked them back up after school, and Candice had changed clothes and returned to the barn, she had to force herself from the car.

"Mom, can we just clean the stall and leave?" she asked. Kate and Taylor were nowhere around.

"You don't want to ride?"

"Not really." Even though Colin had gone to his friend's house and he wasn't there to complain, she still didn't feel like riding. "The footing is probably rock hard anyway."

"It should be fine," her mother said. "It's been thawing all day. What's really going on?"

"I'm tired of riding alone. It's no fun." She felt lonely, left out by the Horse Club.

"I think not riding tonight is fine. Since tomorrow is Saturday, you can ride then, when it's warmer." Her mother touched her shoulder. "Call Kate tonight to find out when they're planning to ride tomorrow."

"I'll do that." It wasn't as though they would call her. Candice needed to stop the way she was thinking. The girls had their way of doing things and who was she to ask them to change? She was lucky they rode with her whenever they did.

Candice was almost finished cleaning the stall when Kate and Taylor walked into the barn. "Kate!" Candice silently scolded herself for appearing too eager to see them.

"Hi Candice," Kate replied. "Are you riding tonight?"

"I wasn't planning to. It's too cold."

"If you don't mind, I'll exercise Spirit tonight, instead of tomorrow."

Candice's heart grew heavy. At least she'd get to ride him on a Saturday without having to wait until Kate finished. "What time are you riding Razor tomorrow?"

Kate and Taylor whispered back and forth, making Candice wonder what they were saying. Were they discussing a time, or were they discussing if they wanted to ride with her at all. Candice's mom always said never to whisper in front of people. Now she knew why. It made her uncomfortable.

"One o'clock," Kate said.

They didn't ask if that worked for Candice but that was okay.

"Do you want to ride with us?" Kate asked.

"Yes!" Again Candice scolded herself for seeming too eager. She was just glad to have someone to ride with and didn't care if they thought she was needy.

“We’ll meet you in the ring at one,” Kate said. She followed Taylor into the tack room to gather their saddles and grooming supplies. When they returned, Kate set her saddle on the rack outside Spirit’s stall.

Candice tried not to show her jealousy. She wished Kate would focus on Razor and leave Spirit to her. Why was she doing this?

Maybe she didn’t think Candice was a good enough rider to lease her precious pony. Wait until she saw her trot. Kate might change her mind.

“Candice?” Taylor asked as she clipped the cross ties on Frankie. “There’s a Valentine’s party at Irish Spring Stable next Saturday night. Do you want to meet us there?”

They didn’t ask her to go along with them, but meeting there was better than nothing.

CHAPTER NINE

Candice appreciated the opportunity to ride in the arena with Kate and Taylor. She missed being with them more than she realized. At least they were including her and treating her almost like a member of the Horse Club.

She had to admit, with the girls nearby, it was easier to tolerate the lunge line lessons. She didn't have to deal with it long today, though. To her surprise, halfway through the ride, her mom unclipped the line.

"Go ahead, trot," her mom said.

A small squeal of excitement escaped Candice's lips. Finally, she'd be able to ride with the older girls.

She asked Spirit for the trot but he only walked faster. Maybe he didn't think she was ready for such an accomplishment. She tapped him with her crop, which she'd had plenty of experience using by now.

He trotted five strides at most. It was hard to maintain a pace when he kept breaking gait.

"Can I help you?" Taylor asked.

"Sure," Candice said, trusting that Taylor had a plan even though she couldn't imagine how Taylor could help.

"Follow me." Taylor urged Frankie ahead of the pony, then turned in the saddle to look back at Candice. "I'm going to trot. Spirit will want to keep up with Frankie, so be ready. If I go too fast, let me know."

"Okay." Candice was more than ready.

"Shorten your reins," her mom reminded.

Candice listened and slid her hands forward on the reins. She couldn't wait to trot with Taylor. She'd been looking forward to this day for a long time.

"Here we go," Taylor said. She cued Frankie and he started to trot.

Spirit perked his ears. It didn't take much to encourage him to trot after his friend. Candice counted the two beats of the trot repeatedly in her head to maintain the rhythm. It wasn't so difficult anymore.

"You're doing it!" Kate yelled. She sat on Razor in the middle of the arena, watching Candice.

Candice smiled but she didn't want to answer. Talking would mess up the counting she was trying to focus on.

Frankie started moving too fast. Spirit happily followed. Candice tried to keep up with posting the trot but she'd never trotted this long, so she was starting to grow tired. She missed a couple of beats, bouncing around.

"Slow down, Taylor," Candice's mom said with urgency in her voice.

Taylor glanced back and brought Frankie to a walk. "Someone's been practicing." Taylor looked proud.

Candice nodded. She gasped to catch her breath. After a few minutes of rest, she said, "I'm ready to trot again."

They played follow the leader for a while. It was great practice because Candice didn't have to steer. She had the fence on one side, and Spirit wanted to go wherever Frankie went. He just plopped along behind them, nice and steady.

At the end of the ride, Candice's mom let her ride around the entire arena alone, without following Taylor. What a thrill. Candice felt her confidence increasing, almost soaring above the clouds.

When they were finished, the three girls gathered in the middle of the arena to hang out. Finally, Candice felt like one of them.

"Do you want to go on a trail ride?" Taylor asked Kate.

"No thanks." Kate leaned forward on Razor to

hug his neck.

Taylor frowned at her friend. "I noticed you spent a lot of time in the middle watching Candice and me ride. Is everything okay with Razor?"

Kate shrugged. "Sure, he was fine today."

"Did you canter him?"

Kate didn't answer. Candice figured that meant she hadn't cantered. Kate and her new horse didn't seem to be getting along well.

Whatever happened, Candice hoped she'd get to keep leasing Spirit.

Kate sat up, looked at Candice and Spirit, and smiled. "I would take Spirit on a trail."

A surge of anger shot through Candice. Whom did Kate think she was to take Spirit away whenever she wanted to ride?

Candice was supposed to be leasing him. She had been looking forward to grooming Spirit after her ride today. She planned to take her time brushing out his tail and braiding it. Her mom said she didn't mind waiting, and Colin had stayed home with their dad, so they didn't have to worry about him growing bored. This was her one day, a warmer one at that, to pamper her new pony.

"How would you do that?" Taylor asked. "You have Razor to take care of."

Kate looked at her mother sitting in the Lexus. She was most likely working on her laptop as she usually did. "My mom could take him back. She always wants me to go on a trail ride, so I bet she'd untack Razor."

"She wants you to take Razor on a trail, not Spirit," Taylor said.

Kate glanced at the Lexus again. "You heard my mom. She told me not to do anything other than basic riding until Layne can give me a lesson. Taking him on a trail ride isn't basic."

Taylor raised her eyebrows. "Kate?"

"Let's talk about Razor later." They both looked at Candice.

Suddenly Candice felt like an outsider.

"Would you mind if I ride Spirit on a trail?" Kate asked.

Of course Candice minded, but how was she supposed to tell the truth without Kate getting mad? Technically he was Kate's pony. What could she say?

"Let me ask my mom," Kate said. She rode Razor over to the fence near the Lexus. She waved her hands to get her mother's attention. Her mom glanced up and the window closest to the arena slid down.

"Mom, can you take Razor back to the barn for me? I want to ride Spirit on a trail with Taylor."

Her mom didn't seem to notice the pout on Candice's face. How could they think this was fair? Maybe no one cared about her feelings. Perhaps she needed to accept that.

Apparently it didn't matter if Candice was the one taking care of Spirit, cleaning his stall before school on freezing cold mornings. Who cared if she had to work harder to finish her homework, so she could clean the stall again in the afternoons?

Candice tried to be understanding but right now she was mad.

"Sure, I can take Razor back to the barn," Mrs. Patrick said.

Kate hopped off Razor and ran up her stirrups. Kate's mom climbed from the Lexus, walked down the small hill, and entered the arena. Kate handed him off to her.

"Thanks, mom." Kate didn't seem to notice that Candice hadn't moved.

She was still sitting atop her pony, unable to dismount. How could they not see how unfair this was?

Candice's mom appeared at her side. "It's okay. We can come back tomorrow to groom him. I'll take you to the mall instead."

Candice looked down at her mother, feeling a lot of warmth toward her. She was always there to save the day when Candice needed her. She slipped off her pony and reluctantly handed over the reins to Kate.

Right now Candice was so angry she barely liked the other girl.

CHAPTER TEN

"Do you think that was mean to take Spirit on a trail ride?" Kate asked as they crossed the grassy bridge over the bubbling creek.

"I wouldn't say mean. Maybe insensitive," Taylor said, twisting back in the saddle to hear what Kate was saying.

Kate glanced away. "I don't mean to be like that. It's not about Candice; it's about me wanting to go on a trail ride."

Taylor stared at her for a moment. "It's about you being afraid to take Razor on a trail ride."

"Ouch. You hit a person where it hurts," Kate said.

Taylor shrugged. "It's the truth. When is your lesson with Layne?"

Kate wished it were sooner. "Not for two weeks. She's still on vacation, and then she's booked solid with lessons." How was she supposed to ride Razor in the meantime? Taylor was right; she was afraid of him. She liked the challenge of having a bigger horse, to an extent, but not the bucking.

"You'll be fine to work him on the flat as long as you make sure he's ready to canter before you ask," Taylor said. She placed her hand on Frankie's rump while she leaned back to talk. "The only reason he's bucking is because it's cold outside and he's feeling playful. You have to vary your work more before you canter."

Taylor was right, but that didn't drive the fear away. Kate wished it were that easy. "What I don't understand is that it was cold and windy when I tried Razor out before I bought him. He scooted a couple of times from wind gusts but he didn't buck. The weather was worse then. What's the difference?"

Taylor squinted in the winter sun. Whenever she grew quiet, she was searching for a logical answer. Finally she said, "They probably worked him more because he was in the therapeutic riding school. I bet they rode him six days a week."

True. With the holidays and the cold weather, Kate hadn't ridden him as much as she should. It was difficult to take gymnastics two days a week, complete the mound of homework she always had, and ride two horses.

"I need to keep exercising Spirit to keep him in

shape," Kate explained. She ran her hand along his fuzzy neck. He was so soft.

"Sure, but you didn't need to take him on a trail ride today. Candice did a fine job riding him. She's coming along well with her trotting."

Was Taylor taking Candice's side?

"That's not cantering him around the arena, or really working him to keep his joints supple," Kate said. To be honest, trail riding didn't do that, either. Basically she wanted to relax by riding on the trails with a friend, and she wasn't about to bring Razor out here again, or at least anytime soon.

"You need to let go of Spirit."

Kate started chewing on her lip. Why was everyone against her?

When Kate didn't respond, Taylor twisted around in the saddle more. "Kate?"

"I know you're right, but how do I let go?"

Taylor's face softened. "My mom would say to take a day to feel jealous. After that, every time you feel jealous, let it blow away in the wind."

Her friend's wisdom always amazed her. "That sounds good but I don't know."

"You have to make a commitment, a decision to let go."

Kate wasn't sure that was possible. Every time she saw little Candice loving on Spirit, her heart ached. She missed feeling like she couldn't show affection to her own pony. Maybe leasing him out was a bad idea; perhaps selling him was a better choice. The lease agreement was for three months, and then they could either sign for a longer period, or end the lease. But three months seemed forever.

A barking dog caught Kate's attention. Sure enough, it was the Rottweiler. He yelped and ran through his invisible fence, which was obviously not strong enough to convince him to stay in his yard.

Ears pricked forward, Spirit stopped dead in his tracks. The scary dog bolted toward them, causing Frankie to spin in place and Spirit to turn and run. Kate sat back to stay on him. He bolted down the path from which they'd just traveled.

Up ahead there was a low-hanging tree branch.

"Whoa, Spirit," Kate said but he didn't listen. She pulled and released his reins but he wouldn't stop. At the last minute she ducked to dodge the branch.

The dog ran behind them.

"Whoa," Kate said again. The dog caught up with them, and while Spirit was running, the dog lunged at him. Spirit scooted to the side to dodge the dog. "Go home!" Kate yelled. Unfortunately the dog didn't listen. "Now!" The dog still ignored her.

Quickly Kate thought back to when the dog had listened to Taylor. She had said it in a deeper, more commanding voice. And without fear.

"Go home," Kate repeated, this time in a lower

voice. She sounded more confident despite her pounding heart.

The dog stopped. He watched her closely, as if trying to decide if she really meant what she said.

Spirit stopped running the moment the dog backed off. He was huffing and puffing, and he seemed thankful the dog had stopped chasing him. Spirit was out of shape, and with his thick winter coat, he was hot.

Kate pointed to the dog's yard.

To her surprise, the dog turned around and headed home. After ten feet he stopped to look back at Kate again.

"Go." She jabbed her finger in the air with a little more emphasis. She wasn't playing around.

The dog tucked his tail between his back legs and scurried home. He sat just outside the invisible fence, watching them.

Kate rode back to where Taylor and Frankie were standing. She had to laugh at Taylor's expression. Her mouth was hanging open in surprise.

"Way to go, Kate," Taylor said after she appeared to recover from surprise.

"Thanks." Kate smiled. That small success with the dog felt good. They rode by him and he continued to study them. This time, though, he stretched out on the ground.

Feeling confident, Kate offered to lead the way,

but Frankie pushed ahead. That was okay, because she had a bigger stride than Spirit anyway. Kate held back and let Frankie pass.

They rode far enough down the winding path to feel safe from the dog, and then Taylor twisted around in the saddle. "You really took charge of the situation. All I did was watch."

Was Taylor feeling guilty about not helping? "You were fine," Kate said. In fact, Taylor had done exactly the right thing by letting Kate take charge for once. Kate relied on her friend too much sometimes.

"I've been thinking," Kate said to Taylor's back. She'd already turned around in the saddle to face where they were walking. At this point the trail got tricky with several shallow ditches to cross.

Once they picked their way through the rough area, Taylor twisted in the saddle again. "What have you been thinking about?"

"About canceling the lease with Candice." There, Kate had voiced what was most on her mind. She gazed out at the bare trees to avoid Taylor's direct stare but curiosity took over. She wanted to see Taylor's response.

Taylor's eyebrows shot upward. "You would actually sell Spirit?"

Kate slid her hand across his soft neck and rubbed him. "It might be easier than seeing Candice ride him."

"Maybe. But wouldn't you miss him?"

Kate nodded. "Of course I would."

Taylor shook her head in disbelief. "I know I suggested before that you consider selling him, but I'm not so sure. I have to ask this. Would you rather sell him, so you don't have to share, than to let a little girl, who really wants a pony, love on a horse you don't have time to ride?"

The way Taylor said it made Kate feel selfish. Then again, maybe Taylor was right. Perhaps she was being selfish.

Kate shrugged. "I wouldn't have said it that way, but yes." She inhaled a deep breath in order to discuss the painful subject. "Or I could sell Razor. We aren't bonding anyway."

Taylor rolled her eyes. "You think keeping a pony that can't jump anymore is better than owning a horse that you'll eventually learn to ride? I'm sorry, but I think you're letting your jealousy take over your common sense."

Kate pouted. "Well you don't have to be so rude about it."

"I'm not trying to be rude. I want you to think about what you just said." Taylor turned back around on her horse, picked the path to the left, which led back to the barn, and then twisted around in her saddle again to face Kate.

Kate wished her friend hadn't turned back around because she looked angry. Taylor never got mad at her.

"Remove yourself from the jealousy and really think about this. I mean, Razor is a good horse. You'll be able to jump him in shows."

Kate had to admit the truth no matter how hard it was. "I'm afraid of him."

"That will go away once you get to know him better. You used to be afraid of Spirit."

"That's not true," Kate said defensively. "Unless you count jumping him over bigger fences." Taylor wasn't being fair.

"Yes you were. You were afraid to canter, afraid to trot over poles, afraid to canter a jump, afraid to trail ride. This is a phase. You'll get over it."

Taylor was right. Kate had been afraid of those things at first with Spirit, all except trail riding. "I wasn't afraid to trail ride."

"You had me lead, like you do now with Razor." Taylor's face softened. "I'm not trying to be mean, but I want you to realize you'll be fine with Razor eventually, just like you are with Spirit now."

Thankfully the barn came into view. Kate couldn't wait to end this discussion.

"I'll think about what you said, but I'm still considering ending the lease with Candice."

"That's your choice, but I encourage you to think about it for a week or so." Taylor's face relaxed and she didn't look angry anymore. Disappointed maybe. "Don't make a fast decision. And talk to your mom about it."

The horses' hooves clicked on the asphalt of the parking lot. Candice had left the barn already; her parents' car was gone. Thank goodness. Kate wanted to think about Spirit, about what to do with the lease, without the interference of seeing Candice. Kate really did like her, which made the decision harder.

They hopped off their horses and led them into the barn. Taylor stopped short, almost causing Kate to run into the back of Frankie.

"What are you doing?" Kate asked. She followed Taylor's gaze to the dry erase board. Candice had written in large letters, *I love my pony Spirit.*

Kate's heart ached. Why was Candice making the situation more difficult than it already was?

"Kate, don't let that bother you," Taylor said. "Candice probably feels we were unfair to take Spirit on a trail ride. We didn't bother to ask how she felt about it. Her feelings are hurt."

Kate didn't care about anything other than the ripping pain in her chest and fighting off the urge to cry. Maybe she *should* sell Spirit.

CHAPTER ELEVEN

Candice hadn't seen Kate and Taylor all week. They didn't call to say when they were riding, or to ask if Candice wanted to join them. She was lonely and bored.

This morning was no different. Kate must have decided not to ride Spirit today, or if she was planning to ride, Candice had no clue what time. She peeked into Razor's stall but he wasn't there. She glanced into Frankie's stall. No horse. The girls had to be out riding somewhere. Candice decided to ride alone again.

She couldn't help but worry, though, about the Valentine's party tonight. Did the girls still want her to meet them there? They hadn't mentioned it since the day they'd invited her.

Lonely, Candice tacked up and rode Spirit to the ring. She was able to ride now without using the lunge line at all. After she warmed him up she asked for the trot.

From the far end of the arena, she caught a glimpse of the Horse Club girls through the trees. They were riding in Taylor's field and looked to be laughing and galloping around. Candice couldn't help but feel envious.

Why couldn't she ride with them?

What hurt the most was they didn't ask if she wanted to join, didn't appear to care how left out she felt. Instead of becoming friends with them, the distance seemed to be increasing between them.

A flash of a galloping horse caught her attention. It was Taylor and Frankie. Candice noticed that Kate wasn't participating with Razor; instead, she was sitting on him watching. Kate was probably afraid, but at least she was riding Razor outside the arena.

"Good job!" Candice's mom said, bringing Candice's thoughts back to the present. "Your trotting is really going well.

"Thanks, Mom." Her mother's positive words were exactly what she needed to hear.

After Candice finished riding and she'd put Spirit back in his stall, the quiet barn began to bother her. Other than Candice and her brother, there were only adults around. They were friendly enough, but it didn't make the loneliness go away.

She picked up the pitchfork and began to clean the stall. Thankfully it wasn't too dirty today. In all honesty, she was tired of cleaning a stall twice a day when it was cold enough outside to freeze water buckets almost solid. Of course, the hard work would be worthwhile if she had other kids to ride with. Her dream of joining the Horse Club seemed unlikely.

"Candice, can't we leave now? I'm cold," Colin whined, entering the barn. He'd been playing with his little cars on a patch of ice in a ditch and had reached his limit with waiting in the cold.

"Me too," Candice said. "I'm almost finished with the stall. I have to crack the ice in the water buckets before we leave." Maybe Candice should give up on the lease and do them all a favor. Kate didn't want her around Spirit anyway. She didn't seem to appreciate all the work involved and the good job Candice was doing to take care of *Kate's* pony. Yes, Spirit was Kate's pony. She'd made that quite clear.

"I'll finish as fast as I can, Colin. Hang in there. You're doing a good job being patient." It felt good to compliment her brother. Their father had a meeting today. Unfortunately, Colin had to spend Saturday morning at the barn, so she could indulge in her horse passion. What a brother.

She tossed Spirit's blanket onto his back and fastened the buckles. If she had to give him up, she'd miss him. A tear slid down her cheek. She wiped it away before it froze on her cheek.

Candice gave Spirit a pat.

She took the hammer from the hook outside the stall and began to crack the water buckets so he'd have water to drink. Too bad the buckets were only half full. She pulled off her gloves to connect the hose and turn it on. Dripping water covered her red, chapped hands, reminding her again of all the work she was doing without any acknowledgement or appreciation from Kate. Taking care of Spirit was part of the lease, so she shouldn't have expectations of Kate. Still, praise was always nice.

The water trickled from the half-frozen hose. She pulled on her thick gloves but the slight warmth didn't come close to thawing out her hands. It was too cold out here.

To tolerate the weather, she needed to think pleasant thoughts while the buckets filled. The Valentine's party tonight popped into her mind. She loved dances. She had fun shopping for a dress with her mother, but now she wasn't sure she should go. Kate and Taylor had invited her to meet them there, but that wasn't the same as going with them. What would Candice do if they ignored her?

She would probably know people since she used to ride at Irish Spring Stable, but it would be more fun to actually go to the party with someone.

Candice planned to watch her friend Ashley Carpenter's lesson today at Irish Spring Stable, so she could ask around to see if any of her casual friends were coming. Maybe Ashley had changed her mind about going to the party. Her parents had made plans for tonight, but Ashley was trying to get out of them. She said she already had a dress to wear because she'd gone to another Valentine's party. Candice hoped her friend went, so she'd have someone to hang out with.

Who knew if Kate and Taylor would even talk to her? They seemed more interested in boys, Josh Thompson to be exact. If Candice saw him today, she planned to mention Taylor liked him. Thinking of them dancing together was a gross thought, but if that's what Taylor wanted, Candice could deal with it. He was nice enough, kind of picky about the horses, but she could see why Taylor thought he was cute.

Candice liked his sunny blond-streaked hair. He was too tall but he was strong. He was good at handling the skittish horses.

The water was almost to the rim of the bucket so she turned off the hose. Candice disconnected it and rolled it up. She'd have to go home and change out of her riding clothes and into something warmer. She'd have just enough time to eat lunch before heading off to Ashley's lesson.

"See you later, Spirit." Candice patted him. She dug a horse cookie out of her coat pocket and pressed the treat to his lips. He graciously accepted it, then begged for another one. Candice laughed.

"You're worse than my dog. I don't have any more cookies." She kissed his fuzzy cheek. Even though he was a lot of work, he was fun too. Maybe she should keep him, even if she had to ride alone.

As she was leaving the barn, Kate and Taylor stopped their horses in the parking lot and dismounted.

"Hi Candice," Kate said. "We're going to my house to show each other our Valentine's dresses. Do you want to come?"

Candice didn't know what to say. They were asking her to join them?

"We'd love to see what you're wearing," Taylor said.

"What color is your dress?" Kate asked.

Candice looked at her mom, who winked. Thankfully the other girls didn't see it. Colin noticed the wink, and Candice hoped he wouldn't comment in front of the girls.

"Red," Candice answered. "My dress is red."

Kate slid off Razor. "I have a pair of heart earrings you can have. They'd look cute on you."

Why were they being so nice? Were they just excited about the party tonight?

"If you want to come over, we can fix your hair," Kate said. "I have all kinds of bows and ribbons."

Candice had mixed feelings. Part of her wanted to go with the girls to feel like she belonged, but the other part, the stubborn part, wanted to push them away. They hadn't been all that nice to her lately, so why should she go to Kate's house? Besides, she had plans to watch Ashley's lesson. Then something her mother once said popped into her mind. Sometimes it took a while to fit into a new group of friends. She said it could be rough for a while, but if Candice remained nice and kept trying, they'd eventually include her. Was that what was happening?

Even though she hated to turn down their offer, Candice had other plans. "Thanks for asking, but I'm going to Irish Spring Stable today to watch my friend's lesson."

"Why don't you stop by after you're finished?" Kate asked. "I'd love to play with your hair."

Candice glanced at her mom. She nodded her approval, so Candice accepted the offer. Really, what was the worst thing that could happen by going to Kate's house?

"I'm cold," Colin whimpered.

"We're ready, sweetheart," their mom said. "Go ahead and get in the car. We'll be right there."

Confused about what just happened with Kate and Taylor, Candice decided to talk to her mom once they were in the car. She waved at the girls, then climbed in. Her mom closed the door and blasted the heater.

"They're coming around," her mom said,

putting her hand in front of the vent to make sure the heater was blowing hot air. "I knew they would. Just go over there and have fun. Most of all, be yourself."

"But I don't understand," Kate said.

Her mom glanced in the rearview mirror. "You don't have to figure it out. If I had to guess, though, I'd say both of those girls like you. Unfortunately, sharing Spirit brings out the competitive, jealous side of Kate. But at her house, you aren't trying to share the same pony. You can just be friends."

They pulled into their driveway. If Candice wanted to be on time to Ashley's lesson, she had to hurry. She changed clothes and grabbed the sandwich her mother had made. Thankfully she made it to Irish Spring in time to help Ashley groom Whisper before the lesson.

Ashley had her horse in the cross ties when Candice approached. She stroked his face and the girls chatted easily for a few moments.

"I'll be back," Ashley said. "I need to get my tack."

Candice nodded. Remembering that she wanted to talk to Josh Thompson, she glanced around, but he was nowhere. She'd have to look for him after the lesson. She couldn't wait to tell him that Taylor liked him. The excitement gave her something to focus on, instead of worrying about going to Kate's house later.

The idea of the Horse Club girls wanting to make her hair cute for the dance still shocked her. All this time she wanted to be included, and now, the thought of going to Kate's house made her nervous. To distract herself, Candice picked up a curry comb and started scrubbing off dirt from Whisper's back.

Her thoughts drifted to the dance again. When Ashley returned with her tack, Candice asked, "Did you get out of your parents' plans tonight? Can you come to the dance?"

Ashley grinned wide. "Yes! I'll be there."

What a relief. Candice would have someone to hang out with in addition to the Horse Club girls.

They talked nonstop about their dresses while they tacked up Whisper. Candice enjoyed chatting with another girl, even if Ashley was a year older. She was still close enough in age that they got along well. Too bad they didn't live in the same neighborhood, so they could ride together. What fun that would be.

"Let's go, Whisper," Ashley said when they'd finished tacking up. She stepped forward, her horse eagerly walking next to her.

When they arrived at the arena, Candice spotted Josh. He was riding one of the feisty horses the stable was trying to sell. Mesmerized by his skill, Candice watched him jump the flighty horse. The landing was rough, the horse shaking his head and dancing around. Despite the horse's behavior, Josh kept perfect form over the jumps. Too bad Kate wasn't here to watch how well he handled the horse. He was brave, and most of all, calm.

She wished Kate could ride Razor like that. Fear got the best of her, though.

If things didn't work out for Kate and Razor, would she want Spirit back? That thought created a wave of anxiety in Candice.

Then she got an idea. What if she told Josh about Kate's problem? Maybe he could help her somehow, perhaps by coming to their barn and riding Razor for Kate. Kate would be so grateful to Candice that she'd offer her membership to the Horse Club. Taylor would be thrilled too because she could stare at Josh and watch him ride. Everyone would be happy.

When Josh finished riding, he nodded in Candice's direction to acknowledge her. She waved. As soon as Ashley finished riding and they returned to the barn, Candice would have a conversation with him.

CHAPTER TWELVE

Candice knocked on Kate's door while her mother waited in the car. She reminded herself that being included with the Horse Club girls was what she wanted. She shifted the weight of her Valentine's dress, covered in plastic and still on the hanger, from one shoulder to the other.

Kate opened the door. "You're here." She smiled and looked friendly.

Candice waved goodbye to her mom. She really wanted to climb back in the car but if she wanted to be friends with the girls, then she needed to accept their invitation to hang out with them.

"Come in," Kate said. She opened the door wider. "Taylor just got here."

Candice followed her upstairs and into a pink and white bedroom. She wasn't sure what she expected, but this room seemed like a little girl's room. She liked it immediately. It was fairly neat and tidy, but there were stuffed animals piled on the bed. Off to the side, a doll with messy black hair sat next to an overstuffed elephant. Cute.

The furniture was white wicker. Candice had a dresser just like Kate's.

"Let's see your dress," Taylor said to Candice eagerly.

Candice stood there in the center of the room. She wasn't sure she fit in with these girls, even though they were being nice.

Taylor scooted closer. "Let me help you." She held out her hand and Candice gave her the dress.

Taylor pushed up the plastic. "Oh, this is beautiful. I love the dark red." She ran her hand over the taffeta dress. "I want one like this. I especially like the silver sequins." She ran a finger over the glittery sequin waistline and shoulder straps.

Candice began to relax. Maybe being here wasn't too bad.

"I love it!" Kate said. "You have good taste in clothes."

Candice's mom had picked it out, but she wasn't about to admit the truth. At least Candice had helped with choosing it. Her mother usually bought all Candice's school clothes, for which Candice was grateful. She enjoyed going to the mall with her mother, but she needed help picking out the right outfits.

"My heart earrings will look awesome with your dress," Kate said. She dug through a white jewelry box until she found the earrings. She held them up. "Do you like them?"

Candice nodded.

"Then they're yours." Kate handed them to her. "Go ahead, wear them. If you need help, just ask."

Candice could put her own earrings on but she was grateful the girls wanted to help. She leaned over to look in the mirror above the dresser. Kate was right, the earrings would look good with the dress.

"Thanks," Candice said. Those were the first words she'd spoken since she'd entered the room. She was still nervous and feeling shy.

Kate and Taylor showed her their dresses. They were nice, but to Candice's surprise, hers was nicer. Not that it mattered. No one had to know they bought the dress on sale for a great price.

Kate sat down at her make-up table. She pulled open a drawer and pulled out a bag of bows and ribbons.

"Let's see what will go with your dress. Do you have a favorite?" Kate asked.

Candice stepped closer. She fingered several of them but one ribbon in particular stood out. It matched the sequins perfectly.

"Good choice," Kate said. "If you sit here, I'll work on your hair."

Candice's mom had insisted Candice bring her own brush. She handed it to Kate, who got right to work brushing Candice's shoulder-length, sandy-colored hair.

"Your hair is so soft," Kate said.

The girls spent at least forty minutes taking turns playing with Candice's hair. When they finished, she looked in the mirror. She was speechless. At first she was concerned they'd make her hair look like a little girl's, but they hadn't.

"Wow," Candice said. She looked older than she was.

"How about some make-up?" Kate asked.

How was she supposed to tell the older girls that her mother didn't allow her to wear make-up? That would make her sound like a baby. She thought about letting them do it anyway, but her mother would tell her to wash it off. When Kate and Taylor saw her later at the Valentine's party, they'd wonder why she removed it. She supposed it was better to tell the truth.

"I can't wear it," Candice said.

"I can't wear some of it, either," Taylor said. "It makes me break out."

Taylor had misunderstood what Candice was trying to say.

"No, I mean my mother won't let me wear make-up. She says I'm too young," Candice explained. Her mom said telling the truth made a person feel better, but Candice was feeling miserable.

"No problem," Kate said. "I'm only allowed to wear a little bit on special occasions."

It was a relief that they hadn't automatically considered Candice a baby. It was also good to know that Kate's mom didn't want Kate to wear make-up, either. Candice looked at Taylor for approval.

Taylor shrugged. "Actually, I only wear lip gloss. My mom has to convince me to even wear a dress to church. It's not fair because all the other kids wear jeans, but she's old fashioned. She thinks it's disrespectful to God or something. Personally, I don't think he cares one way or the other as long as I'm there."

Candice laughed. She was finally starting to relax.

She wanted to tell Kate and Taylor about her conversation with Josh Thompson, but decided against it. She wanted them to be surprised tonight.

CHAPTER THIRTEEN

Kate hurried across the poorly lit parking lot with Taylor, both of them about to freeze. They'd left their coats at home to avoid wearing them over their dresses. Kate regretted their decision now but it was too late to do anything about it. As they approached the rented building, Kate could hear the music thumping through the doors. The dance was going to be so much fun.

"I'm nervous," Taylor confessed.

Kate stared at her friend, although she could barely see her face in the dim lighting. "You're never nervous, not even at horseshows."

"Sure I am. I just never show it." Taylor stopped in front of the doors. "I mean, what good does it do?"

Kate wasn't sure she believed Taylor. She was always so brave. "If that's true, then why voice your nervousness now?" Kate asked.

Taylor shrugged. "What if Josh asks me to

dance? What do I do?" Taylor twisted her fingers around each other.

Kate grinned. So guys made her best friend anxious? She rather enjoyed learning that Taylor was human, instead of an overly confident, competitive machine. Before tonight, Kate would have bet money that Taylor didn't know what the words nervous or fear meant.

"Why are you grinning at me like that?" Taylor asked.

Kate ignored the question and opened the door. "If he asks you to dance, no big deal." It was her turn to be the confident one. She never imagined how amazing it would feel. If she could capture the same attitude when she rode Razor, then he'd probably behave better.

When they entered the room, a familiar-looking woman handed them each a sticky name tag. They wrote their names on it with a black marker. Reluctantly Kate stuck it on her pretty dress. She hoped the sticker wouldn't leave a mark on her dress when it came time to remove it.

They made their way around the room. Kate recognized several girls from the handful of horseshows she'd entered over the years. Horse people knew each other somehow. A few girls she recognized from school, but most of the others were in middle school or younger girls she didn't know.

The center of the room was the designated

dance floor, with Valentine's decorations twirling around slowly from the ceiling. Even though the music was upbeat, no one danced yet.

Taylor nudged Kate's elbow. "There he is, to our right. He's talking to two girls." Kate started to look but Taylor said, "No, don't turn around. That's too obvious."

Wanting to see how good Josh Thompson looked dressed up, Kate fought the urge to glance at him. "What do you want to do first?"

"Let's get some punch," Taylor said. She hurried away from Josh, toward the small crowd gathered at one end of the room. When they reached the long table, decorated in a white tablecloth with pink cutout hearts on top, a woman smiled at them. She dunked a ladle into the bowl of red punch with floating fruit on top and handed each of them a cup.

They stood there and drank their punch, looking around. When Taylor finished, she tossed her cup into the trashcan.

Two girls in fancy dresses were working their way to the punch table. They snickered as they passed Kate and Taylor.

"What were they laughing at?" Kate asked.

"Who knows? Let's see if we can find Candice," Taylor suggested.

"Sounds good," Kate said, still watching the girls. The blond-haired one leaned toward the other, and whatever she said caused the girl to laugh. They both looked in Kate and Taylor's direction.

Kate ignored it at first, but it was bothering her. She tossed her cup in the trash and walked away.

When the girls followed them across the room, whispering, Taylor turned around so fast she bumped into one of them.

"Excuse me? Is something funny?" Taylor asked innocently enough, but the message was clear. Taylor wanted to know why the girls were laughing.

The girl with blond hair stopped snickering but the black-haired one covered her mouth with her hand. Kate could see a smile still on her face.

"Well?" Taylor asked.

The blond girl shook her head.

Kate pulled Taylor away and they found a place to stand by a table near the dance floor. A few daring souls began dancing to a popular song.

Another handful of girls nearby started to whisper and they kept glancing at Kate and Taylor.

"What is going on here?" Taylor asked. "I get the feeling they're gossiping about us."

"Me too."

"I see them at horseshows and they're friendly," Taylor said. "What do they have to whisper about?"

Kate chewed on her lower lip.

Josh walked by and ignored them. He didn't even look their way.

"He usually says hi to me," Taylor said, so only Kate could hear. "I swear, if I didn't know better, I'd think someone told Josh I like him. But nobody knows except you, and you wouldn't do that to me."

Kate shrugged her shoulders. "I get the feeling they're laughing and talking about me too, but I have no idea why. I haven't seen these people in six months at least."

"There's Candice," Taylor said, pointing toward the punch table.

Kate was glad to see her. She waved to Candice, who waved back.

"She looks amazing," Kate said.

"She does," Taylor replied. "And she's always smiling."

"Let's go talk to her," Kate said, leading the way. Unfortunately they had to walk by the giggling girls again. "Ignore them, Taylor." She grabbed her friend's arm to keep her moving in the direction of Candice without stopping.

Taylor squared her shoulders. She passed the girls, and to Kate's surprise, Taylor acted as though they weren't bothering her in the least.

When they reached Candice, Kate gave her a hug.

"This is my friend, Ashley." Candice pointed at a girl standing beside her. "She rides at Irish Spring Stable."

Immediately Kate liked Candice's friend. She

seemed confident and wore a friendly smile. "Do you have your own horse?"

"Yes," Ashley said. They talked about breeds of horses and jumping.

Taylor asked her a few questions and they chatted. Kate could tell Taylor liked Ashley too.

The snickering girls walked by them. They waved at Candice and ignored Kate and Taylor altogether. Kate couldn't help but wonder how Candice knew them. Then she remembered Candice used to ride at Irish Spring Stables.

Had Candice told people how rotten Kate treated her? Was that why the girls were snubbing them?

No, Kate decided. She was worried about nothing. Candice didn't hang out at Irish Spring, and if she did, why would she talk about her? Then she remembered Candice went there today to watch a friend's lesson, probably Ashley's.

Kate began to wonder if she had something to be concerned about actually. Did she treat Candice so horribly that she'd complain to other people?

Involuntarily Kate nodded.

Josh Thompson stopped next to Candice and hugged her. Kate noticed how Taylor couldn't keep from staring at him. She didn't blame her; he looked hot. He had gel in his honey-colored hair and it stood up all over in an adorable way.

How did Candice know him? Was she that well

liked at Irish Spring Stable? Everyone seemed to hug her, or to make a point of talking to her.

Josh glanced at Kate and nodded a hello. His eyes were baby blue, the color of a cloudless sky. She could see why Taylor had a crush on him; he was cute for sure.

Kate smiled back, being careful not to flirt with him. Taylor would disown her as a friend if she encouraged him in anyway.

Then he glanced at Taylor and blushed, his face turning a bright shade of red. From his reaction, he had to know about Taylor's crush. Who could have mentioned it? Kate looked at Candice. Candice didn't know, did she? Kate tried to remember if they'd discussed Josh in front of her. She didn't think so.

Maybe he was turning red because he liked Taylor.

He didn't say hi to Taylor, though. In fact, he barely looked at her. With a reaction like that, it didn't seem likely he'd ask Taylor to dance.

"Have fun, ladies," Josh said. He glanced at Taylor one more time, the red returning to his face, and then he strode off in the opposite direction.

Taylor stared after him. "He's never going to ask me to dance."

"Yes he will," Candice said.

Both girls looked at her. Even Candice's friend seemed shocked.

"I talked with him this morning when I was at the stable watching Ashley's lesson." Candice nudged her friend. "You were cleaning your tack."

Kate was so stunned she didn't know what to say. Taylor seemed speechless too.

Taylor recovered first. "What exactly did you say to him?"

Taylor's tone was a bit cranky, so it wasn't a surprise when Candice took a step back.

"What did you say to him?" Taylor repeated, this time using a somewhat friendlier tone.

"Nothing really."

"Spill it, Candice." The edge was back in Taylor's voice.

"Okay, I told Josh you had a crush on him. I asked if he'd dance with you tonight. I said that you wanted to."

Taylor's jaw dropped. "No. Please tell me you didn't say that."

Candice's eyes were large. She nodded.

Taylor ran off to the bathroom.

"He said yes," Candice mumbled. "And he agreed to ride Razor for you. He said it would be a pleasure."

"Excuse me? Why would he ride my horse?" Kate asked.

"Because you're afraid of him," Candice mumbled again. A group of girls walked by, all of them looking at Kate in an odd way.

Was that why the girls were laughing at her? They knew she was afraid to ride her own horse.

"Did anyone else hear this conversation," Kate asked.

Hesitantly, Candice nodded. "There was a blond-haired girl nearby. She didn't seem to care, though."

That must be the giggling blond who'd been following them around. No wonder they were laughing. They thought she was a chicken.

It was Kate's turn to run to the bathroom.

CHAPTER FOURTEEN

The next morning, Kate rolled her eyes at Taylor. Her friend had been soaring like an eagle all through church, then lunch, and now at the barn. It was already late afternoon and her friend's excitement hadn't worn off.

"I danced with Josh Thompson," Taylor said dreamily for the hundredth time. "He's so tall, so strong, so hot. He felt like a prince, sweeping me around the dance floor."

Kate pretended to yawn from boredom. She was tired of hearing about Josh.

"The slow dance was the best." Taylor sighed and looked upward. Then her gaze met Kate's. "Do you think he likes me?"

"Sure."

"I mean, do you think he really likes me?"

Kate had never seen Taylor act like this, not even after she reached one of her challenging horseshow goals.

"I mean, he asked for my phone number," Taylor said in a soft voice that Kate didn't recognize.

"Yes. And if he calls, then he really likes you," Kate said, trying not to let her true feelings show on her face. She wanted to talk about something other than Josh. She was glad, however, that her friend found a guy she liked so much.

"I'll get to see Josh again today. Wasn't that nice of him to agree to ride Razor?"

It was downright embarrassing. "Um, yeah, sure," Kate said. She didn't like needing him to ride her horse. If she weren't afraid, she could do it herself. Secretly, she did appreciate his offer. She wished she could find a way to allow him to help her without seeming afraid.

Once they had a long talk in the bathroom at the dance, they'd decided not to be upset at Candice for trying to help. After that, the night turned out well, with Josh asking Taylor to dance, and offering to ride Razor. The way he approached the idea of riding seemed friendly without threatening Kate.

"You should let him take Razor on a trail ride. It would be good for your horse," Taylor reasoned. "Josh could give him a relaxing ride, so he behaves when you ride him on the trails."

Why did that make her feel like a child? Obviously Taylor didn't think Kate was a good enough rider to handle Razor on the trails. Her comment hurt. Needing help from a professional, like Layne, was reasonable. Requiring help from someone her own age? That was embarrassing. Okay, Josh wasn't exactly the same age; he was a year older, but still. The idea stung.

"Why are you chewing on your lip and pouting," Taylor asked. "I suggested his help with the trail ride because I thought you'd appreciate it."

"I do, sort of." Kate reminded herself to be honest with her friend. "It just drives home that I'm inexperienced and need another kid's help."

"He's not just a kid, he's almost a trainer."

"But he's not. He's close to our age."

Taylor shrugged. "So what? He can help you until Layne gives you a lesson."

"I guess so. Maybe I could take Spirit on a trail ride, and the three of us can go together." That sounded like more fun than staying at the barn waiting for the two of them to return.

"What about Candice? She's riding with us in the ring, so taking her pony away isn't fair."

Kate frowned. She guessed Candice wouldn't want to wait at the barn alone, either. Was this how Candice felt when they went on trail rides? How unfair. Kate tried to ignore the thought but it was difficult. Her mother always said the truth hurt, and she was probably right.

Kate bridled Razor and left the barn. Candice was in the process of mounting Spirit. He tried to step forward but Candice's mom stopped him. Kate had to admit, they were good at correcting Spirit's manners. He was better behaved. He seemed to thrive with all the love Candice was doting on him, not that that was a bad thing.

Taylor led the way up the hill, Candice last because her pony had the smallest stride. Kate had to admit, Candice was a perfect fit for Spirit, and she took wonderful care of him. Kate twisted in her saddle and watched Candice. "You're doing well with him. And in case you haven't noticed, we are on a trail ride with you. It's a short one, but you are riding by yourself." Candice's mom was far behind them, nowhere near Spirit's head.

Candice glanced back at her mom. Kate enjoyed seeing the girl's face brighten. It was more fun to compliment Candice instead of allowing jealousy to take over. She could have stayed mad about Candice's stunt at the Valentine's party, having embarrassed Kate in front of everyone and making her look like a chicken. But regardless, Josh would show up to ride. Honestly, she was relieved to have help.

When they reached the top of the hill, Kate saw Josh standing on the opposite side of the arena.

"There he is," Taylor whispered.

"Get control of yourself," Kate said. "No guy wants you drooling all over him. Gross."

"You're just jealous."

"Ouch," Kate said. Apparently she was the jealous type.

Josh hopped the fence and met them in the center of the ring. He was dressed in his tight riding pants, a bright blue long-sleeved shirt, and a sleeveless riding vest. Kate had to admit, he was stunning.

Taylor's eyes met Josh's and they wore goofy smiles on their faces. He must have remembered Kate because he turned around. "Are you ready for me to ride this beast?" He rubbed Razor's face.

Beast? Was that a slam, as in *What do you have to be afraid of with this gentle beast?* Embarrassment flushed Kate's face. She wanted to be a confident rider more than anything.

"Sure." Kate dismounted. She needed to let go of her pride and let Josh help her.

He led Razor to the mounting block and swung his long leg around Razor's back with ease. Razor was a fairly tall horse but somehow Josh made him look small.

"What are you having trouble with?" he asked Kate.

"He bucks sometimes when I ask for the canter. He just seems antsy, especially on trail rides."

Josh cued Razor to walk forward, stretching the horse's neck low to relax his back. Razor obeyed immediately. His lumbering walk amazed Kate.

"He feels calm now. Are you nervous when

you ride him?"

The moment of truth was here. She had to admit her fear to Josh and trust that he wouldn't spread it around. She reasoned that everyone at Irish Spring already seemed to know that she was afraid thanks to Candice. But if it weren't for her, Josh wouldn't be helping right now.

Grateful he was here, she nodded. "Yes, I'm nervous."

"What is your worst fear?"

"That he will buck. I'm not sure I can stay on."

"You've already stayed on," Josh said logically. "You said he bucked, and unless you left something out, you stayed on."

That was true.

Josh rode Razor respectfully around the area where Candice trotted Spirit. Her mom was helping her again, but off the lunge line.

Kate watched Razor behave like the perfect gentleman. When Josh asked for the canter, Razor eagerly listened. There was no buck, not even a tail swish. What was Kate doing wrong? Razor was never that good for her. Did her fear really play that important of a role in his behavior? Amazed, she watched every move Josh made.

She could see why Taylor adored him. He was a talented rider. And confident.

Candice was now trotting around the arena by herself. With the use of her cute little crop, the end shaped like a glittery pink heart, she was able to keep Spirit from breaking the trot.

Josh rode for a long while. As the sun disappeared over the far hill, the temperature dipped. It was chilly and yet Razor still behaved.

Just then Razor stopped and perked his ears. He must have heard something in the woods, a deer maybe.

Candice was trotting toward the area where Razor stared. Four deer shot through the small pasture on the other side of the arena fence. In a flash they darted back into the woods.

Spirit stopped dead and raised his head. Then he scooted to the side.

Candice's mom yelled for her to turn him in a circle but Candice didn't hear.

Spirit scooted again and broke into a canter for a few strides. Candice had never cantered before. She lost her balance and tipped onto his neck.

Her mom hurried toward her but it was too late. Spirit broke into a panicked canter, trying to escape what he thought were dangerous deer. Candice lost her balance, and in slow motion, she fell over Spirit's shoulder and landed in a lump on the ground. She cried out in pain.

Kate was probably closest to Candice. She started running and reached her first. She knew not to move her, so she dropped to her knees and rubbed her back instead. Right then, seeing the little girl curled in a ball, crying on the dirt, Kate realized how much the adorable girl meant to her.

"Candice, are you hurt?" Kate asked.

Candice didn't answer but continued to cry.

"I need to know if you're in pain. I know you're scared but try to talk to me."

Candice's mom collapsed by her child's side. "Sweetheart ..."

Josh and Taylor rode over, not too close so the horses wouldn't spook and step on Candice.

"Do we need to call an ambulance?" Taylor asked.

"I'm ... okay," Candice said. Her tears mixed with the dirt on her face.

Kate pulled her sleeve over her hand and wiped the grime from Candice's pink cheek. "It's okay," Kate said. "Just breathe slowly and catch your breath. You're going to be fine."

Candice's mom looked into Kate's eyes. "Thanks."

Kate nodded. Suddenly she felt rotten for how truly horrible she'd treated little Candice. The child met Kate's gaze. Seeing her cry was breaking Kate's heart.

Spirit ran up to them, snorting. Taylor climbed off Frankie and grabbed the pony's reins. "Whoa." She steadied him.

"Why did he dump me?" Candice's voice shuddered.

"There were deer in the woods. I promise, he wasn't trying to hurt you," Kate explained. "He was so afraid he forgot you were up there." Kate rubbed Candice's shoulder. "Are you hurt?"

She shook her head. "I think I'm okay." Candice tried to stand but almost fell. Kate wrapped her arm around the girl's waist to support her.

"Take it easy," Kate said.

Candice's mom hugged her, causing Kate to let go and step back.

"I know you're upset," Candice's mom said, "but if you can, you need to get back on a horse, any horse."

Candice shook her head.

"If you don't, the fear will get worse.

Kate knew all about that, even though she'd never fallen off. To think the fear could intensify if Candice didn't get back on was disturbing. "Candice, trust me on this," Kate said. "You need to get back on a horse now. You don't want to be afraid like I am." Speaking the truth out loud was getting easier. There was nothing to be ashamed of.

"I can't," Candice said. "My legs hurt."

"You're standing so you are most likely fine," Candice's mom said. "I want you to at least sit on a horse, even if it's not Spirit."

"She can sit on Razor. He'll be fine." Why was Kate offering her horse to Candice? All this time she'd resisted sharing with the girl. And why suggest a horse she was afraid of herself? Kate knew Razor was only reacting to her own fear, though, and even if Candice were afraid, Razor would be fine because they'd be leading him. "I promise he'll behave. We'll give you a pony ride."

Candice glanced up at the big horse. "Okay."

Josh slipped off Razor's back. He adjusted the stirrups for Candice so she'd be able to reach them. "Let me give you a leg up."

Candice bent her left knee so Josh could help her. Gently he set her in the saddle.

"Just sit there for a minute and get acquainted with Razor," he said. "When you're ready to walk let me know."

After a moment, Candice said, "I'm ready."

What a brave little girl.

Josh led her around, while Kate walked along the left side of the saddle, and Candice's mom walked along the right side. After two trips around the ring, Candice wanted to steer Razor without help. Josh let go of his hold on the reins but he stayed close.

After a few more trips around the arena, Candice was ready to dismount.

To Kate's disappointment, Candice said, "I'm not going to ride Spirit anymore."

Wasn't that what Kate had wanted all along? Unfortunately, now that it was too late, Kate changed her mind. She wanted Candice to continue leasing Spirit.

CHAPTER FIFTEEN

The next morning Candice showed up at the barn to clean Spirit's stall. She had no intention, however, of riding him again.

"Candice, this is a lot of work for a pony you don't intend to ride," Candice's mom said.

"I love him, Mom. I just don't want to be on his back."

"Oh, honey," her mom said. She gave Candice a loving hug. "I think you enjoy riding him; it's falling off you don't like. There's a big difference."

"You can't fall off if you don't ride," Candice reasoned.

Her mom leaned over and looked her directly in the eyes. "You need to get back on him. After a couple of times, the fear will lessen."

"The woods are right there," Candice said. "A deer could pop out at anytime and spook him again." It wasn't worth the risk.

"There is danger in everything you do."

Candice shook her head. There was no arguing with her mother; she always had an answer. No matter what her mom said, though, she wasn't getting back on that pony.

"We can't keep taking care of a horse we don't ride," her mom explained. "It's too much work."

A tear slowly wove its way down Candice's cheek. She didn't bother to wipe it away. Why couldn't her mother be supportive? If Candice enjoyed being around horses, why couldn't she take care of one for fun? Why did she have to ride?

Candice had a sudden urge to take down the Valentines she made, which were still hanging on Spirit's stall. The one that hurt the most to see was the small poster that read *Be My Valentine Horse*. Giving him up was going to be difficult.

"I'm cold," Colin whined. "Can't you hurry up?"

Candice felt pressure from everyone. All she wanted to do was wrap her arms around Spirit and stay there with him all morning. Unfortunately she had school. How was she supposed to sit down all day on her sore bottom? In Candice's book bag, her mother had packed a small pillow to sit on, but how embarrassing. Everyone would ask what happened and she'd have to tell her classmates she fell off her pony. No thanks.

"I want to leave," Colin said.

"I'm hurrying. Leave me alone," Candice

snapped, but then felt bad. Her misery wasn't her brother's fault.

His bottom lip poked out.

"I'm sorry," she said. "I didn't mean to yell at you. I still have to break ice and refill the water buckets, and I have to clean the manure out of the paddock." Normally cleaning the small paddock didn't take long.

"I'll do the water if you do the poop," Colin said. "That part's disgusting."

"Deal," Candice replied. She dragged the muck bucket and pitch fork out the open doorway at the back of Spirit's stall. Spirit stood nearby, happily munching his hay. Candice scooped up the first pile of frozen manure and it sounded like rocks when she tossed it into the muck bucket. She'd be glad when spring got here, but who knew if she'd still have her pony? If she didn't agree to ride him, she knew her mother would stop the lease.

Candice hurried to finish her barn work because she was cold too. When she was done, off to school they went.

It was a painful and emotionally awkward day. She didn't like reliving the details of falling off Spirit. Every time one of her friends asked, it brought the experience back to her mind. By the time she returned to the barn that afternoon, her fear of riding Spirit was worse than ever.

The Horse Club girls were tacking up, getting

ready for a ride. Candice watched from the stall she was cleaning. A tiny part of her wanted to join them, but mostly she wanted to keep both feet on the ground.

"Are you going to ride with us," Kate asked. She caught Candice peeking through the bars of the stall.

"Not today." To Candice's surprise, Kate actually looked sad. Falling off Spirit seemed to have bonded them. It was a little late for that because Candice would likely have to let him go. Then a disturbing thought jolted her. If she had to back out of the lease, whom would Kate find to ride Spirit?

"I'm sure you're sore from falling off, but you really need to get back on Spirit," Kate said. "Besides, he needs the work."

"Maybe you should ride him." Candice hated to suggest that Kate take over, something Candice had resisted up to this point. But what choice did she have? She didn't want to ride him.

"No thanks. I have to exercise Razor." Kate looked almost tempted to accept the offer, but then she patted Razor's neck. "I need to focus on him. That leaves you to ride Spirit."

Candice glanced away. What she was about to say was hard. "I need to end the lease. I'd love to keep Spirit as a pet, to take care of him, but my mom says he's too much work unless I'm riding."

"Simple," Kate said. "Ride him, and then you'll get to keep the lease."

Candice crossed her arms. "Like I said before, I can't."

Kate stepped closer to her, leaning against the stall. "I know all about fear. At some point you have to face it."

Candice shook her head.

Razor reached out and rubbed his face on Kate. Kate giggled but made him stop. "Razor's getting antsy, so I need to go." When Razor tried to rub on Kate again, she scratched the itchy spot on his face to satisfy him. "I'll come up with an idea. Trust me; we can work through this."

Candice didn't think so.

"Why don't you come up to the arena?" Kate asked. "Josh is going to ride Razor for me again. It might help to watch. And believe me, if anyone knows what you're going through, it's me."

Candice knew her mom would support her decision to observe. More than anything, her mother wanted her to continue to ride. "Thanks. I'll ask my mom to drive me up there."

"See you soon." Kate led Razor through the barn aisle and disappeared out the door.

What harm would it be to hang out with the Horse Club? There was no pressure to join anymore.

CHAPTER SIXTEEN

The week scooted by at warp speed for Kate. She had testing at school, a mess of homework, gymnastics twice a week, and Razor. Her life was a little overwhelming right now, but she enjoyed her after-school activities. They made everything worthwhile.

Josh had stopped by to ride Razor a couple of times, which, of course, made Taylor happy. Kate would never admit that she had a crush on Josh too. She enjoyed watching him ride Razor and appreciated all his help. He did a marvelous job with her horse. If anything, he convinced her that her own fear was the cause of Razor's behavior. Razor hadn't bucked, scooted, or spooked since Josh had started riding him. Kate felt her confidence in her horse increasing.

Today, with Josh's help, she was going to ride Razor. This weekend she had a lesson scheduled with Layne, so if Kate could ride this afternoon to regain some trust, she'd be able to make better use of the upcoming lesson.

Then it hit her. That was the answer to Candice's problem. If she could take lessons from Layne, then she could continue to lease her pony. But then Kate remembered the reason why they decided to lease Spirit in the first place. Her mom had lost her job and they couldn't afford to take lessons at Irish Spring Stable anymore.

Kate would have to come up with another plan. This called for a Horse Club meeting.

"Taylor," she called out as they made their way up the steep hill to the arena, Kate walking instead of riding. Taylor twisted around in her saddle. "Can you meet tonight?" Kate asked. "We need to come up with a plan to help Candice keep Spirit."

"I thought you wanted her to quit leasing him, so you could have him back?" Taylor asked in her usual annoying, direct way.

"I changed my mind after she fell off Spirit," Kate said. "Seeing her on the ground made me realize how much I like her."

Taylor seemed surprised but pleased. "Maybe we should ask her to join the Horse Club."

Kate chewed on her bottom lip. "She needs a horse to ride before she can join, and right now she says she's never riding again." The idea of having another member in the club somehow seemed threatening. It had always been just Kate and Taylor in the club. Would having a third member change things?

"Maybe if we ask her to join, she'll ride again," Taylor suggested.

Kate guessed that was possible. Was she ready to invite Candice to be a member of the Horse Club? She wasn't sure.

"Kate? What do you think?"

"I'll ask her." But first she needed to think about it.

They reached the top of the hill and entered the arena. Josh was standing in the middle, talking to Candice and her mother. Kate's mom was waiting in the Lexus parked nearby.

"Hi Kate," Josh said as he started to walk toward her.

Taylor flashed Kate a stern look, claiming ownership of Josh. Kate didn't intend to steal her best friend's guy, nor did she think Josh was even attracted to her. Although she could be wrong. Now that she thought about it, he had been helping her a lot lately. He'd said hi to her without acknowledging Taylor. Just the thought of Josh liking her made her heart rate speed up, not a good situation.

Kate waved at him.

"Are you ready?" he asked.

"Yes." Fear or not, she was ready to ride her horse again.

Josh helped her mostly with the trot. He gave her a lot of advice, all good, and it seemed he was giving her a lesson. He wasn't as detailed as Layne was, but he was helpful. Whatever suggestions he made, she tried them. Razor was behaving, until they asked for the canter. Again, Razor raised his head and swished his tail.

Kate backed off and walked him. "That's what he does before he bucks."

Josh rubbed his chin with his right hand. He appeared to be thinking. "Razor's doing that because you're clamping down on him by squeezing your whole leg around his barrel. That's how a mountain lion would attack his back. I'm surprised he only bucks. A lot of horses would panic."

"So he's reacting to me?" She figured that, but she hadn't understood why.

"Yes. You're also leaning forward onto his neck, tense and pulling back on the reins while you ask for the canter. Just relax."

Kate tried to listen to Josh. She worked Razor for a while, the focus on fixing Kate's negative riding pattern. After she cantered successfully several times without Razor reacting defensively, she brought him to the center of the ring so Josh could jump him around a course.

"Are you ready to ride the monster?" Kate laughed. She'd come a long way by being able to joke about the circumstance. She realized there was nothing wrong with Razor. If she fixed herself by dealing with her fear, he'd behave for her. That alone made her feel better. She wasn't exactly sure how she'd fix the problem completely, but at least she was working toward an answer. She hoped Candice was willing to have the same goal with her riding.

"I'm ready," Josh said, rubbing Razor's face as he always did before he mounted. Kate caught the warm look he sent Taylor, who was giving Frankie a short break from all the groundwork they'd just finished. Of course, Taylor missed the affectionate look, so she'd still blame Kate for trying to steal Josh's attention away from her.

Kate slid from her horse. She joined Candice on the bleachers, and together they watched the others ride.

"You know, I've been thinking," Kate said. "How would you like to join the Horse Club?"

Out of the corner of Kate's eye, she noticed Candice's jaw drop. "Really?"

Kate nodded.

Candice bounced sideways on the bleacher, giving Kate a tight hug, and then she slowly scooted away. "Oh, wait. I can't join because I won't be riding anymore."

"Maybe that's temporary."

"I don't think so. A deer could show up at

anytime, and I could fall off again." Candice sounded so grown up.

"That's true, but once you learn how to ride really well, you'll be able to stay on him when he spooks."

Candice wrapped her arms around her upper body. Kate suspected it wasn't because the girl was cold, but that she was protecting herself from the memory of the awful fall.

"Why don't you think about it?"

Candice remained silent for a long moment. "Okay."

In the meantime, the Horse Club planned to meet tonight to come up with a plan to get Candice back on Spirit. "Do you want to ride Razor today?" Kate asked. "You did such a great job with him last time."

Kate thought Candice would smile but she didn't. Instead, she kept her arms crossed around the middle of her body.

"You really need to get back on. It's important."

"Okay. I'll ride Razor but not Spirit."

That was a start.

They watched as Taylor and Josh began to jump their horses. Flawlessly, Razor trotted over everything Josh asked. Then Josh had him trot the first jump and canter the second. They looked amazing. How did Josh make it look so easy?

Before long, he was cantering a course. Again, they looked professional and sleek. Kate longed to ride like that. Seeing how calm Razor was with Josh gave her hope.

When he finished, they put Candice on Razor to cool him down. Kate led her around while Josh offered Taylor a few pointers with her jumping.

"I like Razor. He's so big," Candice said as Kate walked a large circle.

"He is that. That's why I was afraid of him."

"Aren't you scared anymore?" Candice asked.

Kate glanced up at her. "I don't think so. Well, maybe a little." She might do flatwork but no way would she trail ride or jump. Not yet.

They walked several times around the circle, and then Taylor rode up to them on Frankie. "Can Josh take Razor on a trail ride with me?" Taylor tipped her head to the side and gave her a cute puppy dog look.

"Begging doesn't become you," Kate said.

"Please."

Kate preferred to get back on her horse and ride him down to the barn, but Taylor looked pathetic. Her friend wanted to spend time with cute Josh, and Kate didn't blame her.

"I guess so," Kate said.

"Thanks!" Taylor raised her voice so Josh could hear her. "She said yes."

He smiled and headed toward Kate and

Candice, obviously wanting to get on Razor again.

"It's time to dismount, kiddo." Kate helped her off Razor. It was a long way down for her.

After Taylor and Josh left on the trail ride, Kate felt left out. While she didn't want to ride on the trail, she didn't want them to leave her behind, either. She glanced down at Candice. Was this how she felt every time they took off to ride without her? How horrible.

"I'm sorry, Candice."

Candice scrunched her face. "For what?"

"For all the times we rode off without including you. It stinks."

Candice's eyes widened and she hugged her, catching Kate by surprise. Hesitantly, Kate wrapped her arms around her young friend.

"I don't want to hurt you anymore," Kate said. "Please keep riding Spirit."

Candice shook her head. "Sorry, but I can't."

CHAPTER SEVENTEEN

Later that evening Kate and Taylor held a Horse Club meeting.

"How can we get Candice to feel confident enough to ride?" Kate asked.

Taylor shrugged. "I don't know. You're going through the same thing. What's making you ride again?"

Kate might be experiencing something similar to Candice, but Candice's fear was worse. At least Kate would get on her horse. Falling off had to be horrible.

"Seeing Josh ride Razor has helped," Kate said. "It made me realize that my horse isn't wild, that I am the one causing his behavior."

Taylor crossed her legs and leaned back against Kate's white wicker dresser." What if you rode Spirit in front of her?"

"That might make her jealous enough to ride," Kate joked.

"I don't mean ride him to cause jealously. I meant for you to show her he was safe."

That might work, but Candice was afraid of deer in the woods. They usually came out at dusk. "I could ride in the evening when the deer come out."

"He'll spook," Taylor said. "You won't fall off, but if Candice sees him react to the deer, that will scare her more."

True. "Candice shouldn't ride at dusk then," Kate reasoned. "If she avoids the problem, until she becomes a better rider, then she'll be fine."

Taylor's expression became animated. She always got excited when they solved problems. "Yes! That's perfect. But how do we get her back on to begin with?"

"I don't know."

Taylor drummed her fingers against her thigh. "I got it. We can give her a pony ride on Spirit. She's open to being led around on Razor."

Kate shook her head. "If I were her, I'd be afraid to ride in the arena again. That's how fear works. The accident happened there, so every time she sees those woods, she's going to relive her fall."

"What about Spirit's paddock?"

"What about it?"

Taylor rolled her eyes. "We can give her a pony ride in Spirit's paddock. It's a small, safe space."

"Perfect. Then what? How do we transition from the paddock back to the ring?" Kate asked.

Taylor shrugged. "I have no idea. We can worry about that later."

Kate chewed on her lower lip, working it back and forth. That usually helped her think better. "She needs a lesson, maybe when Layne comes to help me. But her mom lost her job."

"She had to quit lessons at Irish Spring," Taylor said. "That's why she's leasing Spirit to begin with."

Kate pulled a shaggy, overstuffed dog onto her lap. She'd had the stuffed animal since she was five years old. Whenever she needed help figuring out a tough problem, Shaggy Dog usually helped.

She thought hard for a few minutes. "My mom might pay for her lesson. We want to lease Spirit because of time issues, not because of money. It would be worth it for us if she continued to lease. That way I can keep my pony. We won't find anyone who does a better job taking care of him."

"That sounds like a logical plan, if you think your mom will agree," Taylor said. "Do you think one lesson will make a difference?"

"Probably not. We could try to earn money to help pay for more," Kate suggested.

"How?"

"We could blow snow off driveways, or walk dogs. I enjoy taking care of animals." Kate had always wanted a pet, but for some reason her mom never wanted one.

Taylor's face lit up again. "Good idea. We could make flyers and put them in mailboxes in our neighborhood." Taylor began tapping her leg again. It was annoying when she did that. "Can you present the idea to your mom tonight?" Taylor asked.

"Yes," Kate said. "Layne is coming Saturday, so that would be a perfect time for her to work with Candice."

And that's exactly what happened. Kate's mom agreed to pay for a few lessons as long as the Horse Club worked to help earn money. Kate and Taylor made flyers and passed them out. Together they'd already earned forty dollars.

Thankfully, Candice agreed to ride Spirit in a lesson.

Saturday arrived fast. They were at the barn, getting ready for their lesson. The plan was that Candice would ride first, so Kate could help her with whatever she needed. Then, toward the end of Candice's lesson, Kate would return to the barn to tack up Razor.

"I'm nervous," Candice said.

"I can understand that. I'm nervous too," Kate told her.

Candice looked surprised. "I thought you said you weren't worried anymore."

"I changed my mind," Kate said. "That's how fear works. It comes back whenever you think you've gotten rid of it."

"Will it ever go away?" Candice asked.

"Sure. I used to be afraid to jump Spirit but not anymore. Last year we competed over fences at a fairly big show." Kate loved that memory, that accomplishment. "Of course I was nervous about being at the show, but that's normal. I wasn't afraid to jump, though."

"Did you win?"

"Actually, I did. My mom always told me to hold onto my dreams and never let go. I listened and practiced jumping until I lost my fear. The secret is to jump only half of what you do at home, so the fences at the show look like nothing."

"I can do that," Candice said. "Maybe Ms. Layne will put me back on the lunge line."

"Sounds like a good plan. Taylor always says to trust Layne because she's the professional. Maybe we should both listen to that advice."

"Deal." Candice made a fist and bounced her knuckles off Kate's.

"Let's go. Layne is always on time," Kate said, encouraging Candice to lead Spirit out of the barn. "I'll walk up to the ring with you."

"Thanks."

To Kate's surprise, Candice stood on the mounting block. She was going to ride Spirit up to the arena? Apparently her fear was limited to riding in the ring. Spirit tried to move forward but Kate stopped him. Candice hesitated, inhaling a long breath before she slowly stuck her boot in the stirrup.

"You can do it," Kate said. "Don't think too much, just take one step at a time."

Candice swung her right leg behind the saddle. She sat tall on Spirit. "That wasn't so bad."

Kate smiled. "Ready?"

Candice nodded. Instead of letting Kate lead her, she nudged Spirit to walk. "At least the deer aren't out now. My mom says they come out early morning or late evening."

"That's right." Kate hoped that would make a difference with Candice's success.

Too bad Kate's own fear wasn't that easily addressed. The time of day didn't change anything for her.

They made it to the arena without a problem. Candice appeared confident but Kate could see the tension in her body. She was a brave girl. Kate hoped she'd be that courageous when it was her turn to ride.

Layne was waiting for them. She stood in the middle of the ring, talking to both moms. Kate would love to hear what they were saying, but when they approached, the adults stopped talking.

Layne walked up to Candice and Spirit. "I'm

Layne. I hear you're Candice and you are leasing this fine pony, Spirit."

Candice appeared shy, smiling but not saying anything.

"We're going to start off on the lunge line to see what you need help with."

"You know I fell off, right?" Candice asked in a small voice.

"Yes. I promise we'll take it slowly. You'll be fine."

Kate found the words encouraging, even for herself. Layne projected such confidence that worries seemed to disappear. Almost. She was still concerned about cantering and jumping. And trail riding of course.

As the lesson progressed, Candice seemed to calm down. Kate noticed firsthand how the simple gesture of relaxing your body made a huge difference in how your horse reacted. Spirit's whole body seemed to loosen up once Candice relaxed, and he appeared to enjoy the ride. That was a learning opportunity for Kate.

When Layne asked Candice to halt, she unclipped the lunge line.

"I don't think I'm ready," Candice said, her lower lip quivering.

Layne placed her hand on Candice's knee to reassure her. She'd done that many times before to Kate.

"You'll be fine. I'll stay close," Layne said.

Candice remained quiet. She looked like she wanted to cry but she did as Layne asked. Again, Kate admired the girl's bravery.

"Go ahead and trot. I'm right here."

Candice continued to walk Spirit.

"Candice, I'm so close to you I can reach out and grab his reins if I need to," Layne said.

Layne's words seemed to convince Candice because she cued Spirit to trot.

"You're doing marvelous. Look at you," Layne exclaimed.

A small smile escaped Candice's lips.

Relieved Candice was enjoying the lesson, Kate left the arena to tack up Razor. Her belly tightened into several knots. She wasn't sure she could follow through with the ride.

CHAPTER EIGHTEEN

Instead of riding Razor to the arena alone, Kate decided to lead him up the hill. She was safer on foot than on his back. She hadn't realized how much she relied on Taylor, by always following, by always having someone to ride with. She'd forgotten what it was like to ride by herself. Again, she thought about Candice. On the days Kate and Taylor rode without her, Candice probably felt lonely. How sad.

With each minute her fear increased. She could turn around and head back to the barn. It would be no big deal.

Now was her chance to have Layne's help, though. She'd catch Kate's mistakes and Razor would have no need to act out. He wouldn't buck with her riding instructor around. With that thought, she took one step after another toward the ring. She could do this. If little Candice could ride Spirit again after a fall, then Kate could ride Razor after a buck.

She reached the top of the hill way too fast. Candice, with a smile on her face, was cooling out Spirit. She wasn't on a lunge line anymore, so it must have gone well.

Kate led Razor into the arena, half tempted to quit the lesson before it began.

"Kate," Candice exclaimed. "I trotted off the lunge line."

"That's impressive. Way to go." Kate reminded herself that if Candice could face her fear, so could she. For the first time she realized the two of them had something in common.

Kate rather liked that thought. What amazing progress she'd made, from the first day Candice bounced into the barn ready to take over Spirit. The little girl was perfect for him.

"It's your turn, Kate." Candice rode over to her and held out her knuckles to tap Kate's.

"You're right." Kate could do this. Razor had been perfect for Josh all week. He'd been wonderful for her too, once Josh pointed out what she was doing wrong.

Candice and her mom left the arena with Spirit. Razor whinnied after them.

"You're okay, Razor," Kate said. She led her horse to the mounting block. Just before she climbed on, she said a little prayer for safety. She used to do that sometimes before she rode Spirit.

When she finished, she placed the toe of her boot in the stirrup and mounted.

"Kate," Layne said as she approached. "I want you to remember something. The challenges you have faced until this point have made you who you are today. Razor will make you a better rider tomorrow. That is part of learning to ride."

Kate looked down into Layne's eyes, trying to ward off the sting of tears.

"Razor is a good horse," Layne said. "I wouldn't have encouraged you to buy him if he weren't."

Unable to speak, Kate nodded.

"We are going to take it slowly, but I'm going to push you some. That's how you'll get over your fear," Layne said. "Go ahead and walk around the arena."

Kate did as Layne suggested. When the time came close to cantering, though, Kate's fear increased. She tried to remember to focus on positive thoughts. So far Razor had behaved well and listened to every cue she gave him.

"Go ahead and canter."

Kate chewed on her lower lip. Breathe. She had to remember to breathe.

"Kate, ask him to canter."

She thought about all the help Josh had given her. She sat back and tried not to clamp her legs around Razor. She asked for the canter and was relieved when he behaved wonderfully. She reminded herself to relax. That was the key to a successful, uneventful ride.

"Perfect! You are doing a great job."

Kate smiled. It felt good to canter Razor without him tossing his head. He really was awesome.

His stride was long and lumbering. Relaxed. She could do this. Correction, she *was* doing this.

Layne had her work Razor in circles, then straight, then more circles. They did plenty of serpentines at the trot, and changed directions often.

"The secret to riding Razor in the winter is to keep his mind busy. He's somewhat young. You either need to vary your workout when you ride him, or work him six days a week."

Exercising him six days a week was out of the question. With Kate's busy schedule, there was no way she could ride him that often.

"Most of all, relax and be creative," Layne said. "Don't just trot him around for ten minutes and then expect him to behave at the canter. That's too much to ask right now." Layne stood in the center of the arena, her eyes never leaving Kate. "Don't think of trotting as simply something you have to do, think of it as challenging him. Put his mind to work."

Kate listened while she rode.

"He spends most of his day in a stall. He's used to more turnout, but unfortunately, there isn't much pasture he can graze on in your neighborhood. You might want to cut his feed down too."

Layne gave her a brief lesson on feeding horses. "Make sure he has plenty of hay. Chew time for him is important."

Kate continued to ride, with each new exercise building her confidence. By the time Layne wanted her to canter again, Kate felt more relaxed. Razor obeyed immediately, no games or bucking. They did so many transitions, Kate was relieved when Layne allowed her to canter for a longer period.

When the lesson was finished, Layne asked Kate to walk in a circle around her. "I don't want you to trail ride for a while, at least not on him. If you can take Spirit out on the trails occasionally, that would be good for both of you."

How would Candice feel about that? A quick movement from the bleachers caught Kate's eye. She hadn't noticed before but Candice had returned to the arena to watch the lesson. She was giving Kate a thumbs-up to show her approval about taking Spirit on the trails. They were working together as a team.

Kate felt lighthearted and peaceful for the first time since Candice started riding her pony. Kate might own him, but Candice was his new partner, his new mommy.

"And I don't want you to jump Razor without me here," Layne continued to say. "I can come back next weekend, but call if you need me earlier."

Layne's support removed a lot of fear from Kate.

"Thanks, Layne." Kate knew she'd be fine until her next lesson. Layne had taught her ways to handle Razor, ways to encourage positive behavior in him.

"Think about dividing each ride into sizable chunks that you can handle," Layne advised. "First focus on walking only. Don't worry about the trot until you are begging for it. Same with the canter. Don't even think about jumping; we'll take the same approach with it later."

Kate could handle that.

"Ride the moment, one stride at a time," Layne continued. "That's the thing with fear. The more you worry about it, the more it grows into a huge monster. With the technique I gave you, it gives you control over the worry. This works on anything you're afraid of. Break it down and focus on accomplishing one step at a time. Practice this and it will get easier. I promise."

Kate nodded. Layne walked over to Kate's mom and started talking to her. While they weren't looking, Kate headed toward the gate. She wanted to ride Razor down the hill, back to the barn, by herself. She didn't need to follow Taylor and Frankie as she usually did.

Candice surprised her. "Kate, wait up. I'll walk

with you."

Candice fell into step next to her, and together they headed down the hill.

"Candice," Kate said, "I owe you an apology for how I've treated you."

Candice looked up, a slow tear streaking its way down her reddened cheek. The girl had sat there through Kate's lesson even when she was obviously cold.

"I'm sorry too."

"What do you have to be sorry for?" Kate looked down at the girl, who was trying her best to stay caught up with Razor's big stride.

"Because I made it hard on you. I wanted to belong to the Horse Club so badly that I pushed myself on you."

Candice's apology felt good. It was interesting. Kate no longer considered Candice a little girl. In some ways she acted older than Kate did.

"Will you keep leasing Spirit?" Kate asked.

"I don't know," Candice said in a serious tone.

Kate's heart almost stopped beating.

"Got you," Candice teased, chuckling. "Of course I'll lease him."

Relief washed through Kate. "Please don't scare me like that again." When Candice grinned, Kate started to laugh. "Now that you're riding again, do you want to join our club?" Kate asked.

"Yes!" Candice stopped walking and began to

bounce in place.

It felt good to invite her to be a member. "Welcome to the Horse Club then. You can have my pewter necklace until I order you one. Congratulations."

Candice smiled wide. "Thanks. The best reward of all is keeping Spirit."

"And that's why the two of you are a wonderful match," Kate said. "He needs you."

Candice looked up at her with wide eyes.

"Spirit is yours for as long as you want." To Kate's surprise, the words were easy to say.

ABOUT THE AUTHOR

Lisa Morgan started riding horses when she was in the third grade. She competed on the Hunter Jumper circuit, and eventually became a riding instructor. She has three kids, but only one has inherited her love of horses. Through their experiences, and from many hours spent at the barn, Lisa came up with the Horse Club books and the Shackleford Banks Series.

She hopes you continue to enjoy her books. Happy reading!